Secret Admirer

New York Times and USA Today Bestselling Author

CYNTHIA EDEN

PROLOGUE

Alice May barely recognized the woman in the long, white dress. The silk seemed to stretch for miles and miles, and she'd never felt anything so soft against her skin. Her hair had been artfully styled, her makeup carefully applied. Everything was ready. *She* was ready. Her hands tightened around her bouquet—a bouquet of blood red roses.

The wedding would start any moment...

Or, at least, it would start once her groom arrived.

Alice swallowed.

Her bridesmaids were dead silent behind her. When word had first reached them that Hugh Collins hadn't made it to the little chapel on the edge of Savannah, Georgia, they'd just all laughed and said he must have partied too hard at his bachelor party.

He'd be there.

He wouldn't miss his own wedding day.

The door opened. She spun around, her heart jerking in her chest. "Hugh—"

Hugh's brother Jonathan stood in the doorway. His dark hair was no longer perfectly in place. Instead, it stuck up at odd angles, testimony to the fact that he'd been shoving his fingers through it again and again.

Jonathan's gaze — the same battered gold as Hugh's — swept over the room. He jerked his head toward the avidly watching bridesmaids. "Give us a minute, would you?"

Oh, God. Hugh wasn't coming. He'd said he loved her, but he wasn't coming. He'd changed his mind.

After casting her sympathetic glances, the bridesmaids filed out. The door closed behind them with a soft click. And Alice realized she was twisting her bouquet too hard in her hands. Rose petals had fallen to the floor. They almost looked like drops of blood. "He's not coming." Her voice was soft, sad.

"I can't get him on the phone. I had a neighbor check his house. Hugh isn't there…but, the cops were."

Her head whipped up. Fear raced through her. She forgot about the chapel full of people. Forgot about the growing fear that Hugh didn't love her as much as he'd promised. She bounded toward Jonathan. "Is he okay?"

Oh, God, they'd need to check the hospitals. Right the hell away.

"The cops are searching for him, too."
Jonathan swallowed and his gaze darted from
hers. "The neighbor—Sherry something—she
said the cops wanted to arrest him."

A cold chill slid over her skin, but Alice
heard herself give a too-high peal of laughter.
"That's ridiculous. Hugh doesn't even get traffic
tickets. Why would he possibly be arrested?" He
was an engineer. A volunteer firefighter. The guy
was *good*. Dependable.

But Jonathan's face remained tense. He drew
in a deep breath, and his gaze slid back to her
face. "Has he ever…said anything to you about
our dad?"

"Your dad?" Her eyes widened. "He died
when you were kids. Hugh barely remembers
him."

"Right." Jonathan nodded, but his stare had
become hooded.

He's not telling me everything.

"Jon?" Alice whispered. "What's
happening?" Because he knew more, she could
feel it.

Jonathan shook his head. "We should leave. I
don't want you here if…" But his words trailed
away.

"I can't leave my own wedding!"

A rough exhale came from him. "There isn't
going to be a wedding. The cops think Hugh is
on the run, and they are coming *here*. I don't want

you caught in this madness. You need to get out of this place before it becomes a circus."

He wasn't making sense. Nothing was making sense. Her right hand held her bouquet, and her left grabbed the train of her dress. She hurried to the door just as it flew open.

Heather Hollow, her maid of honor, stared at her with wide, stark eyes. "I just heard — on the news — " But she stopped, as if she couldn't say more.

"What?"

Heather just stared at her.

"Heather! Tell me! What did you hear?"

"Th-there's b-been an accident. Just down the road...A blue Mercedes SUV flipped. It was being chased by police cruisers..."

Her heartbeat was suddenly far too loud. "Hugh drives a vehicle like that."

Police cruisers.

The police had been at Hugh's house. A blue Mercedes had flipped.

She shoved past Heather. Rushed down the hall. Dropped her bouquet as she ran. Guests saw her. They called out, their eyes flaring in surprise, but Alice didn't stop. She rushed to the front of the chapel.

For such a small chapel, there were so many people crammed in there. She hadn't wanted to get married in that place. She'd just wanted to run away with Hugh. Only the two of them.

Forever. But Hugh had insisted on taking their vows in front of friends and family. He'd been so excited.

She shoved open the chapel's door. The sunlight hit her, too bright and hot. She was sweating in her beautiful gown, and Alice could hear the scream of sirens. She could also smell smoke in the air.

She started running, not even caring what she looked like. Hugh was late for the wedding. Too late. He was never late. An SUV just like his had been in an accident, and she could see the smoke and flames filling the air. So close to her. She rounded the corner, and there it was. *His* SUV. She knew it was his because she could see the hiking sticker on the SUV's bumper. The burning SUV.

Alice screamed and ran forward, but hard hands grabbed her and shoved her back.

One of the uniformed officers barked, "Ma'am, no! This scene isn't safe!"

"That's my fiancé's SUV!" Alice yelled back at him. "Where is Hugh? Where is—"

An explosion rocked the street. The blast was hard enough to send chunks of the SUV flying into the air. Hard enough to send her sprawling back onto the concrete. The skin scraped off her palms, and her dress twisted beneath her.

The uniformed cop reached down for her, and she could see the horror on his face. A terrible combination of horror and sympathy, and she *knew* he was going to say something that would wreck her. She wanted to beg him to stop, wanted him to —

"He was in the vehicle, ma'am. I'm sorry."

***

Alice stared into the mirror. A one-way mirror in a police interrogation room. Right after the uniformed officer had told her that Hugh had been in the burning vehicle, Alice had been taken from the scene. She'd been crying, been fighting to get to the SUV and Hugh, but the cops had pushed her in the back of a patrol car. They'd taken her to the station. Left her in this room.

Shock had moved in. A numbness that seemed to fill her every limb.

As she stared at her reflection, Alice realized that she didn't look like a blushing bride any longer. Mascara had smeared, and it lined her eyes, giving her a raccoonish appearance. Her dark hair had come out of its careful twist, and her white dress was stained with soot and dirt. Blood had dried on her hands. And Alice just kept thinking...*This can't be real.*

The door opened. Finally. She jumped from her chair, part of her thinking it would be Jonathan walking inside...the way he'd done at the chapel. He'd come in and this time, he'd tell her that everything had been a mistake. A big misunderstanding. Hugh was fine. He hadn't been in the burning SUV.

But Jonathan wasn't there. A blond man with a hard jaw and glinting eyes stared at her. She could have sworn there was anger in his gaze. He wore a dark suit, and a badge was clipped to his hip.

"Alice May?"

She nodded. Shivered.

"I'm FBI Agent Ryan McCall. I want you to sit down."

The FBI? What? "This...it's my wedding day."

His gaze raked her. "I can get more clothes brought in for you."

She didn't want more clothes. She wanted Hugh.

"You should sit back down."

God! He's not saying this is a mistake.

The chair's legs screeched across the floor as she pulled it back. Alice sat in the chair again, falling too heavily. "Please tell me that Hugh isn't dead."

Agent McCall sat across from her and put a manila envelope on the small table. "Hugh Collins was in the SUV when it crashed. We weren't able to get him out before the fire spread." His lips thinned, then he said, "From what we can tell, he died on impact. The fire didn't take him. Bastard got off easy."

Her breath caught in her throat. She could feel herself choking. Why had he just called Hugh a bastard?

Ryan McCall flipped open the manila envelope. "Do you know this woman?"

Alice stared at the woman in the photo. Dark hair. Wide smile. Heart-shaped face. She looked a little like Alice. "N-no…"

Ryan's mouth tightened. "Her name is Vicki Sharpe. She was in the SUV, too."

"Wh-what?"

"Her dead body was found in the rear of the vehicle. After the fire was extinguished, we discovered her. She'd been stabbed in the heart, just like all of the other Secret Admirer's victims. Because most of the fire was centered near the vehicle's engine and front seat, Vicki was still in fairly good condition for the ID."

A dull ringing filled her ears. Had he just said the dead woman had been in "good condition" — wait, no, surely not. Surely, he hadn't just said that a woman had been in the rear of the vehicle. And there was no way the agent had said that she'd been stabbed.

Her heartbeat came faster. Even harder. Alice struggled for breath. "I don't understand…"

He slid another photograph toward her. "Do you know her?"

Another woman with dark hair. Blue eyes. A small mole near her lips. "I-I saw her on the news." Alice was shaking now. "M-Mary Ellen—"

"Mary Ellen Jones. Another victim of the Secret Admirer."

The killer who'd been in the news. The killer who'd terrorized the Savannah area for the last year. He abducted women, all dark-haired, blue-eyed, unmarried women in their mid-twenties. He kept them for a while...torturing them, then when he was done playing with his prey, the killer would stab his victims in the heart before he dumped their bodies.

The Press had dubbed him the Secret Admirer because a reporter had gotten a tip from an unidentified FBI source—that tip had revealed that the guy stalked his victims before he took them. That he sent them flowers. He talked with them online. He seduced them, and the women willingly left with him. But after he got them, after he took them away...

The women never escaped him again.

More photos were slid toward her. Three more women. "Why are you showing these to me?"

"Because we found jewelry belonging to all of these women...in your fiancé's house."

Alice shook her head. "That's not right."

It couldn't be right. *Please, don't be right. Please.*

"We found blood. The weapons he'd used on them."

Alice put her hand to chest and pressed hard.

"Did you know?" Agent McCall's voice seemed distorted. As if it had come from a great distance.

Alice couldn't look away from the photos. All of the women looked like her. Too much like her.

"Did you know that the engagement ring you are wearing belonged to Mary Ellen Jones? It was her grandmother's. Mary Ellen always wore it on a chain around her neck."

Alice's stomach twisted. She could feel bile rising in her throat.

"The ring is evidence, and I'm going to be taking it."

She was already fighting to get the ring off her finger. Only it wouldn't come off. It had always been a little too tight.

"Did you know he was a killer?"

Her gaze snapped up to lock on the FBI agent. He stared at her with a cold fury.

"Because that's what I can't figure out about you yet, Ms. May. You were closer to Hugh Collins than *anyone* else."

She could barely breathe.

"Did you know what he was doing to those women? Did you know he was torturing them?"

His questions battered at her. "Were you covering for him? Were you *helping* the sonofabitch?"

CHAPTER ONE

She didn't look like a killer.

Zander Todd swept his gaze over his neighbor, knowing that his sunglasses would hide the direction of his stare. Alice May didn't realize that he was watching her. She didn't know that he was cataloging every single detail about her appearance.

Her long, thick, dark hair.

Her heart-shaped face. Her red lips. Her high cheekbones.

Her golden skin.

Her long legs.

Alice May was a looker, a woman who seemed to exude sex appeal. And, if the stories were true, if the FBI was right with their suspicions, she was also a killer. One who had managed to get away with her crimes so far.

"What do you think, Zander?" Alice asked as she stepped away from her flower bed, brushing her hands across her hips. "Does that look okay?"

"Fantastic." He put an edge in his voice, one that she wouldn't be able to overlook. Slightly flirtatious. Admiring.

She immediately jerked her gaze toward him. Her eyes went wide. Her little pink tongue gave a nervous swipe over her lower lip. She was good at that. Good at pretending to be innocent. Uncertain.

But the FBI brass didn't think she was nearly as innocent as she seemed to be.

Alice May's fiancé had been the infamous Secret Admirer. A man who'd murdered five women before he'd been killed.

The case should have been closed. Hugh Collins had died a year ago.

But two months ago, the Secret Admirer had claimed another victim.

Zander stepped closer to Alice. Her scent—light jasmine—teased him. "Have dinner with me tonight."

He'd asked her out three times before. And every single time, Alice had shot him down. She hadn't dated anyone since Hugh had died. Zander knew that for a fact, because the FBI had been watching her. Very, very closely.

Alice sucked in a sharp breath and her deep blue eyes widened. "I…don't think that's a good idea."

"You're seeing someone else. I get it." But she wasn't. Would she lie?

Alice shook her head. "No."

"It's me?" He flashed her a smile. He'd been told he had a good smile. Hell, most women found him charming. Alice didn't seem to be like most women. "Just not that into me, huh?"

"No — you...um, you're very handsome."

He laughed at her words. Zander couldn't help it. She'd just sounded all polite and courteous, like she was worried she'd hurt his feelings. She hadn't. But she was making things difficult. His assignment was to get close to Alice. To get her to trust him. To get her to reveal details that she had never spilled during all of her interrogations.

"Did I say something funny?" A faint furrow appeared between Alice's brows. She wiped her dirty hands on her faded jeans. Jeans that fit her like a second skin and showed Zander that Alice was one very, very sexy woman. Long legs. High breasts. Killer smile. Not that she smiled a lot. In fact, in the two months that he'd been working as a "handy man" in the area, Zander had only been able to coax about three smiles from her full lips.

He stilled his laughter. Gave a rueful shake of his head. "A woman as gorgeous as you probably has men lined up for miles, just waiting for her to give them a second glance."

"I don't date." Her words held a brittle edge. "I...had a bad experience once."

That had to be the understatement of the century, but Zander kept his expression controlled. "I'm sorry." He made his voice gentle. "I didn't mean to—to make you uncomfortable." Time for his exit. If he pushed her too hard right now, Zander knew he'd lose her. He'd come out to her cabin to fix her sprinkler system. A system the FBI had sabotaged while she'd been stocking up on groceries the day before. The fix had taken all of three minutes, but it had given him an excuse to see her. To chat with her.

Spring had finally come to the little mountain town of Sky, North Carolina, and Alice had been eager to start her planting. She'd wanted colors. Flowers. She couldn't have any of that without her sprinkler system... *The FBI made her need me again.*

Zander inclined his head toward Alice. "Have a good evening." Then he turned on his heel. He made his steps slow and certain as he headed away from her. And he counted in his head... *Five, four, three—*

Her footsteps rushed behind him.

"Wait!" Alice's fingers pressed to his arm. A fast touch, and then she hurriedly pulled back.

But he whirled toward her. "Something wrong?"

She rocked onto the balls of her feet. "I didn't mean to hurt your feelings."

"You didn't, Alice." Shit, now he was feeling bad. *It's just a job.* Sometimes, though, when he looked too deeply into her eyes, he could forget that. And he could get lost only seeing...her. "Look, I'm not the kind to pry. Something happened in your past, and you don't want to date. That's your business. I understand."

Some of the tension slipped from her shoulders. She tipped her head back so that she could stare up at him. Alice was close to five-foot-eight, but he skirted six-foot-three. And she was too damn thin. Every time he came to the cabin, he found himself picking up pastries for her. Today, he'd brought three cupcakes. She'd given him a smile as a thank you.

Smile number three.

"Everyone else always pries." Her lashes lowered to shield her gaze. "I don't look...familiar to you?"

"Um, I've seen you off and on for the last two months. You definitely look familiar."

She gave a short, negative shake of her head. "That's not what I mean."

He waited. *Come on, Alice. Make this important move. Do it. Trust me.*

Even though he was lying to her. Using her.

She nodded, then her lashes lifted. "Do you remember the Secret Admirer?"

He rubbed a hand over his jaw. "Wasn't that the guy from Savannah? The one who killed those women?"

A flinch had her whole body jerking. "Yes."

Hard to forget a freak show like that guy. "What about him?"

Her spine straightened. Her chin lifted. "He was my fiancé."

Zander let surprise cover his face.

"The woman in the white wedding dress? The woman who was splashed all across the news and in all the papers? The fool who didn't know her fiancé was a killer?" A smile covered her lips — smile four — only this smile wasn't like the others. This smile was almost painful to see. "That woman was me."

He gave a low whistle. "So when you say you had a bad experience…"

"I mean it." Her smile was gone. "You don't want to date me. You don't want my baggage. You don't want to wake up one day and find reporters camped out on your doorstep because someone in the area realized who I was and tipped them off."

Shit. Alice was trying to protect him?

"You *are* handsome. And you're kind. And you've been an absolute lifesaver to me." Her hand gestured vaguely toward the small cabin that waited behind her. "I swear, every single day, something new is falling apart in this place."

Yes, it was. Because of the FBI.

"If it wasn't for you, I wouldn't have running water, a front door that opened, a refrigerator that worked, electricity that—"

"It's just my job," Zander cut in. The FBI had been sabotaging things left and right, so that she'd have to call Zander. And right then, he felt like a total jerk.

Her gaze softened on him. "You're a nice man."

The hell he was. He was ruthless. He was determined. He was a bit of an adrenaline junkie. But no matter what else might be said about him, Zander *always* got the job done. Zander wasn't the type to hesitate, hell, just ask any of his old Ranger buddies. He was many things, but not *nice.* No one had *ever* called him nice. That title was damn insulting.

"You don't deserve to be dragged down into my trouble." She turned away.

His hand flew out. This time, his fingers reached for her. He caught her wrist, and his hand encircled it. Zander pulled her back toward him, and their bodies *almost* brushed.

Her gaze flew up to his. "What are you doing?"

He shouldn't have touched her. And he absolutely shouldn't be running his thumb along her inner wrist in a soft, sensual caress. Swallowing, Zander let her go as he stepped back. "I like trouble." That was one of the most truthful things he'd ever said to her.

Her lips parted. "You...do?"

"And you're too young to lock yourself away because you had the misfortune to be taken in by some twisted freak."

Her arms wrapped around her stomach.

"I'm not a killer. Hell, if you want them, I can give you references. Can even let you talk to my fourth grade teacher. She'll vouch for me." He paused, then added, "You can trust me." Shit, he almost choked on those words.

"Trust isn't exactly easy for me."

Alice loved her understatements. It was kind of cute.

"One dinner," Zander offered. "That's what I'm asking for. Let me show you that it's okay to live your life again."

"H-how do you know I haven't been living?"

Hell—*fix that blunder.* "When I come out here, you never have friends or family over. You don't even have a dog. You're a beautiful woman, and you're hiding yourself in the mountains. You're hiding from the world. Don't have to be a shrink to realize that." He waited a beat and decided to push more, using info that one of the FBI shrinks had passed along to him. "You're letting him win, Alice. Don't you see that? If you give up your life, isn't it like he killed you, too?"

She held his stare.

Had he pushed too far? Too fast? Dammit. What should he do next? *How to play this, how to —*

"Hugh didn't take my life. But sometimes, it sure feels like he did." She exhaled. "Okay, fine, if my scary past didn't run you off…if you really think you want to date me — I mean, have dinner — then…let's do it."

Hell, yes.

"But…can we have dinner here instead of going out? I'm a really good cook. And I — I don't exactly like being in crowds."

Probably because she was afraid someone would recognize her.

"It's one of the reasons I work from home," she murmured. "I like…quiet. Space."

He knew she worked as a freelance designer. She spent her time creating ad pieces for corporations. And staying *out* of the limelight.

"I stocked up at the grocery store yesterday," Alice continued. "So I've got plenty of food."

Right. She'd been on the trip to the store when her sprinkler had been sabotaged.

"I have steaks." Her words came quickly. "And salad."

He gave her his winning smile. "I have wine."

She didn't smile back, but her eyes seemed to gleam a little more. "Then how about you come back tonight at seven?"

"It's a date." He gave her a little bow, and then he headed for his truck. Zander waited until he was a good distance away from her cabin, then he called his partner. The line rang once, twice —

"Hey, Z. Tell me you made some progress with the target."

Randall Cane's voice filled the interior of the truck as it carried through the Bluetooth system. "I made progress." So why was his gut knotted? "We're having dinner in her cabin tonight."

"Hell, yes. Finally. If anyone could get that woman to lower her guard, I knew it would be you!" Satisfaction deepened Randall's voice.

"It's just dinner," Zander muttered. "Not like she's going to spill every secret she has to me."

"She'd sure as hell better. That's the point of this whole operation. For you to build trust with the target. For her to feel as if she can confide in you. For you to figure out if Alice May is a cold-blooded killer, just like her former lover."

His hands tightened on the wheel, an instinctive reaction. "She doesn't seem the type."

"Yeah, well, don't forget, we found those photos of the vics in *her* apartment."

They had. Black and white photos of the victims had been hidden beneath a floorboard in Alice's closet. She'd claimed never to have seen those photos before. Told authorities that Hugh must have kept them hidden there without her knowledge.

Her fingerprints hadn't been on them. There had been no physical evidence to tie Alice to the murders. There had just been unanswered questions. A whole lot of them...

Why were the photos in her closet?

Why was Alice allowed to live — when she looked exactly like the Secret Admirer's other victims?

Why had the killings all started after Hugh Collins met Alice May?

And even though Hugh Collins was in a cemetery, the Secret Admirer had claimed a new victim two months ago. Julianna Stiles. A woman who appeared eerily similar in appearance to Alice...a woman who'd been found with a knife stabbed in her heart, and rose petals sprinkled around her body. The Secret Admirer's MO. But the Press hadn't gotten wind of the story, not yet. The FBI was trying to keep the murder under wraps. Trying to see if Alice could be tied to that crime...

Trying to see...if Alice had been her lover's partner all along.

Sure, the FBI could be dealing with a copycat. That was one option, but the FBI brass had long suspected that Hugh Collins hadn't worked alone when he'd committed his crimes. And the higher-ups at the Bureau suspected his secret partner was none other than the lovely Alice May.

"If she isn't Julianna's killer," Randall continued, "then she has to know who the fuck is.

No one was closer to Hugh than she was. The killer's identity is in her head, even if she doesn't realize it."

"I'll let you know what I find out. I'm heading back to her place at seven."

Silence. Randall wasn't often the silent type. When he went quiet, it meant he was worried.

"You got something you want to add?" Zander pressed.

"Don't get fooled by a pretty face." Randall's voice had turned brisk. "You know pretty faces can hide sadistic killers. You're the one playing her, not the other way around. Don't forget that shit."

Zander didn't intend to let himself get played.

"She's a job," Randall continued flatly. "Nothing more. Bust her — or find out who the hell was working with her lover. Do whatever it takes, but get the job done."

"I always do."

For some reason though, he had a quick flash of Alice as she stood, wiping her dirt-covered fingers on her jeans. She'd looked so damn innocent.

Was she a world-class liar?

Or one of the Secret Admirer's victims?

He was going to find out the truth about Alice. Even if he had to be a lying bastard in order to uncover her secrets.

CHAPTER TWO

"I brought dessert." Zander flashed a wide smile as he stood at the threshold of Alice's cabin. The smile revealed the two slashes in his cheeks. Not dimples. They were too strong, too hard, too masculine to be dimples.

Her gaze fell to his hands, and she saw that he clasped a bottle of wine in his right hand and an open box of cupcakes in his left. Two cupcakes. Both with chocolate icing.

"I know chocolate is your favorite."

It was. Chocolate had always been her guilty pleasure.

"Thank you." She took the cupcakes and gave a quick nod. Her fingers shook a bit, and Alice hoped he didn't notice. She'd been counting down the minutes to his arrival—both in anticipation and in dread.

She wasn't exactly a pro when it came to dating. In fact, she hadn't dated anyone in almost a year. *Tomorrow will be a year. The dark and twisted anniversary.*

Alice eased out a slow breath. "Come inside." She would not let him see how hard this was for her. She *liked* Zander, dammit. He'd been nothing but helpful. He was sexy as all hell with his dark, slightly curly hair, and his warm, brown eyes. The man had saved her time and time again when her cabin decided to fall apart. The guy was a Good Samaritan.

But then, she'd thought Hugh was good, too.

"I'll put these in the kitchen." She turned away from him. "Give me just a moment." She hurried into the kitchen, trying to get her nerves under control. It was just dinner, for goodness sake. Nothing more.

His footsteps followed her. As quickly as she could, Alice put the cupcakes on the counter. She turned and found Zander standing far too close to her. He leaned toward her, reached out — and put the wine on the counter next to the cupcakes.

Why was it so hard to breathe?

"You're scared." A furrow appeared between his brows. "Did I do something wrong?"

No, he'd done everything right. Including *not* freaking out when she told him about her ex. "I'm, um, a little rusty at dating."

Those slashes appeared again in his cheeks, and his eyes twinkled. "Oh, really?"

"There's…a lot of pressure with dating." She probably sounded like a lunatic. "You know, wondering if you'll connect. Wondering when you'll have the first kiss. Wondering if it will feel right or if it will just be some huge mistake."

His head cocked. "You should stop worrying."

Easier said than done.

"If you're stressing over it, then how about we just get the first kiss out of the way?"

Wait — had he just said —

His hand lifted and curled under her chin. "This way, the pressure will be off."

She hadn't kissed anyone, not since —

"Your mouth is gorgeous, Alice." But he didn't lower his head. He stared into her eyes, and the tension stretched between them. "May I kiss you?"

Her tongue swiped over her lower lip. He was right. They should get this done. Eliminate the pressure. Sounded like a fabulous idea to her. "Y-yes."

His head lowered. He wasn't rushing. Zander took his time, and her whole body stiffened. Not in dread. In anticipation. And when his lips finally met hers, the kiss was tender. Careful. A gentle exploration. There was no awkward bumping. No too-rough press of his mouth. He kissed her with sensual skill, and her lips parted for him even as her hands rose to curl around his broad shoulders. Then his tongue slid into her mouth. And the kiss became a little harder. A little more intense. No, a *lot* more intense because desire burned through her, heating her blood with a sudden, sharp intensity.

Alice found herself leaning toward him. Opening her mouth more. Wanting *more*. A low moan built in her throat and —

Zander pulled back. His gaze seemed to blaze. "Sure didn't feel awkward to me." A pause. "And, sweetheart, rusty is not a word I'd associate with you."

She was breathing too hard. And her fingers were trembling, but not because of fear or nerves, not any longer. Desire beat in her blood. Need had her aching. She wanted to close the distance between them. To kiss him again.

To do one hell of a lot more than just kiss.

"Glad we got that out of the way," Zander murmured, and a twinkle came into his eyes. "And I've got to say, you taste sweeter than cupcakes."

Heat stung her cheeks. She opened her mouth to reply, but her phone rang. Frowning, she glanced toward the counter. Only a few people had her number. Very, very few. The phone vibrated and rang again.

"Go ahead," Zander urged her. "Answer it. I'll get some wine glasses down for us."

Because he'd been the one to fix her cabinet door when it broke last week. He knew exactly where she kept her glasses.

The phone rang again. "Excuse me, just for a moment." She hurried to the phone. *Unknown caller.* That was odd. Alice's finger swiped across the screen. "Hello?"

Silence.

Not unusual. Sometimes, her connection was terrible. She kept meaning to get a landline at the cabin. She walked a few feet and said again, "Hello?"

There was nothing. No response at all. Alice hung up the phone. "Probably a wrong number." She tucked a lock of hair behind her left ear.

He'd gotten down the glasses. "That happen a lot? You getting wrong numbers?"

"No." She headed back toward him. "That's actually my first one since I got the phone." A new phone for her new life. New city. New home.

New Alice.

At least, that had been the plan. Only she didn't feel new. She felt like the same old, hiding coward she'd been since Hugh's death.

Zander opened the wine. Poured her a glass. Poured some in his —

The phone rang again. She glanced down at the screen. *Unknown Caller.* She shoved the phone onto the counter and reached for the wine glass. "Not going to get it this time. It's just a wrong number."

The phone vibrated again. Zander lifted a brow. "How about I answer and tell him to screw off?"

She gave a quick laugh, surprised, but Zander was already reaching for the phone. His fingers slid across the screen, and he put the phone to his ear. "Hello, asshole."

He waited.

So did she.

"Anyone there?" Zander demanded. "Look, since you're not talking, I'll just tell you — I think you have the wrong number. And we're busy, so don't call again." He ended the call. Put the phone back on the counter. Smiled at her. "See, problem solved." A pause. "Now how about that dinner? Then we can enjoy dessert."

***

Alice wasn't alone. The man's voice had been cocky. Too arrogant. He was in her cabin. Night had fallen, and the stranger was *in* Alice's home.

He shouldn't be there. Alice didn't date. Alice didn't have a lover or even a casual boyfriend.

The man shouldn't have been there.

Anger stirred, moving deep inside.

He shouldn't be there, Alice. You know he shouldn't be there. Alice knew the rules. She also knew what would happen if she broke the rules...

***

Thunder rumbled, and a crack of lightning flashed just outside of the window. Alice jumped, startled, and some of her wine spilled over the edge of her glass.

"Sounds like the storm is coming closer." Zander sat near her on the couch. "Guess that's my cue to leave." He gave her a slow smile. "Dinner was amazing, Alice. Thank you."

It had been a good night. They'd eaten. Laughed. Had the cupcakes and a little more wine. He'd told her stories about growing up in the Blue Ridge Mountains, about going to join the Army, becoming a Ranger…

He'd made her feel comfortable. She didn't remember feeling this way, not in a very long time.

Now, he was leaving. Her gaze darted to the window. "Are you okay to drive?"

"Weather forecast said the rough stuff wouldn't be arriving until around midnight. And I'm just down the road." A little laugh. "I actually walked here tonight. My cabin is fifteen minutes north of here."

She knew that. *Maybe* she'd made a point of learning as much about him as she could. With her past, it paid not to be too trusting.

Her gaze slid back to him, and she found his stared on her. Or rather, on her mouth. Immediately, Alice's heartbeat kicked up.

But he just set down his wine glass — still half full. "I enjoyed spending time with you tonight."

Was that it? He was just going to leave?

One brow lifted as Zander asked, "Walk me out?"

"Of course." She put down her wine and scrambled to her feet. He was being a gentleman, not pushing for anything...more from her. That was good. He'd *always* been very courteous with her. Charming. Nice. She hurried toward the door, but his hand flew out and caught hers. He lifted her hand to his mouth and pressed a kiss to the back of her knuckles.

"You spilled a little wine." Another kiss against her skin. "Tastes as sweet as you."

And it was hard for Alice to breathe again. Desire flooded through her. Made her want to taste *him* again. Sweet wasn't the way she'd describe Zander's taste.

Alice didn't move, though. She knew better than to take what she wanted.

He released her hand. Zander's gaze searched hers. "You don't need to be afraid of me."

"I was really wrong about a man before. I don't want to be wrong again." A stark answer.

Zander shook his head. "I want to keep you safe. I don't want to hurt you."

There were lots of ways to be hurt.

"Did he...did *he* hurt you, Alice?" Zander's voice had dropped to a low, lethal tone.

She knew about all the stories that had circulated in the newspapers. It would have been impossible to miss them. Some of the tales had claimed that she'd been Hugh's secret partner. The lover who craved his dark side and helped him commit his brutal kills. Other stories had painted her as the tragic victim. The woman who'd quietly suffered abuse and torture at Hugh's hands. The woman who hadn't been free until he'd died.

The truth, though, was that she wasn't either of those women. She hadn't known what Hugh was doing, and Hugh had *never* hurt her. At least... "Not physically. But he sure as hell did a number on my mind." Hardly the sort of first date talk that Zander typically received.

Why wasn't he running from her as fast as he could?

Zander's head cocked to the right. "You had no idea what Hugh was doing?"

Her stomach twisted. "If I knew, I never would have agreed to marry the guy." Her breath came out on a hard release. "They looked like me." A soft whisper.

Zander's jaw locked. His eyes narrowed.

But she drew herself up, straightening her shoulders. Thunder rumbled again. "Thank you for a lovely night." Then, before she lost her courage, Alice darted forward. She pressed a quick kiss to Zander's lips.

A start of surprise rolled through him. He reached for her, but she'd already retreated. "I think you can beat the rain home." She opened the door. Alice could smell the rain in the distance as she walked onto her porch. The old wood groaned beneath her feet.

Zander followed her out. "I'm not Hugh Collins."

Thank God.

"I'm not some crazed killer who is going to screw with your head. That's not what this is about."

Alice glanced back at him. "Why do you want to be bothered with me and my baggage?" She'd tried to warn him, again and—

He brought his body closer to her. Barely a breath separated them. "It's not a fucking bother. I like you. I want to get to know you."

Her lips started to curl. How long had it been since someone told her that? Since a man hadn't looked at her as if she was the freak in the room? Zander stared at her with a clear, steady gaze, and Alice felt normal. Like she could almost have a regular life again.

His head bent, and he pressed a kiss to her lips. Her mouth parted for him, and his tongue slid inside. The man sure knew how to kiss. She could feel her toes curling in her strappy shoes. Her hands rose and pressed to his chest. A strong, muscled chest. Zander was a big guy, tall and muscled, and there was just something about him…

He slowly eased back. Zander stared at her a moment in the darkness. "I'll see you again soon, Alice." Then he was heading away, striding off the porch and into the night as lightning flashed in the dark sky.

She didn't go back inside, not yet. She watched him, and she became aware of a warmth flaring in her chest. At first, she didn't even realize what that warmth was because it had been so long since she'd felt…

Happy.

***

"I feel like a fucking asshole." Zander stalked the confines of his cabin like a caged tiger, his phone clenched tightly in his hand. "She was sweet and kind, and she was freaking worried about *me*. Trying to make sure I understood what the hell I was getting myself into just by having one date with her."

He couldn't get the image of Alice's smile out of his mind. And the woman's taste...he'd never had anything sweeter. When he'd kissed her, he'd never expected to go from zero to *fuck, yes,* in a matter of seconds. But something had ignited inside of him. A deep, twisting hunger...

For her.

He'd known Alice was attractive. Beautiful. Sexy. He hadn't known that his dick would stand up and applaud the second she kissed him. He also hadn't known...

"I don't like lying to her." It was her eyes. So deep. When she looked at him, it was like she was staring into his soul. "If we're wrong and she wasn't working with Hugh, then I'm just screwing with some innocent woman's head." And he'd *told* her he wouldn't do that. He'd fucking told her! "The FBI has been invading her life—"

"We've got warrants and legal paperwork out the ass to cover us," Randall cut in. "You know I wouldn't have let anyone step so much as a foot into her cabin otherwise."

"We've been *sabotaging—*"

"Five dead women. *Five.* Those five were tied to Hugh Collins. But what about victim six? What the hell about her? Julianna Stiles died two months ago, and everything I've got is pointing to the killer being the Secret Admirer. Only a dead man can't kill."

Sonofabitch. "Alice seems innocent."

"And I told you, don't fall for a pretty face. She got two calls tonight — fucking *two* that traced back to the burner phone that was used to contact Julianna's family."

Every muscle in Zander's body locked down. "What?"

"You know we're monitoring her line. And folks might like to *think* burner phones are untraceable, but that shit is just wrong. We recognized the number that called Alice. Same fucking burner phone used with Julianna. We were triangulating the signal, but Alice was smart enough not to talk long enough for us to get a lock on the caller—"

"I got the second call. I answered it. Not her." Zander just hadn't realized what the hell had been happening. "No one said a damn word to me when I answered. The caller didn't speak."

"Did you hear any sounds? Breathing? Background noise?" Randall pounced.

Zander cracked the blinds and stared into the darkness. The storm was close now, so very close. "No, nothing. But I'll tell you this…when she got the first call, it made her nervous."

"How do you know that?"

"Because when Alice gets nervous, she uses her left hand to tuck her hair behind her ear. It's a dead giveaway. She picked up the phone, all normal, but when the caller didn't speak, she got spooked."

"She *could* have gotten spooked because you were there when her partner made contact."

Randall wanted Alice to be the bad guy. Her being bad would make the case much easier. They could swoop in, lock her up, get her to roll on anyone who'd helped her...and no more dead women. Case finally closed. But Zander wasn't so sure. "I don't think she's a killer."

"And why the hell not? Because she's got pretty blue eyes? Because she can kiss well? And, yeah, we saw you making out on her porch. Gave our surveillance crew quite the show, Z."

"Stop being a dick." A curt demand.

Silence.

Zander sucked in a sharp breath. "She doesn't play as the killer to me. She seems *nice.*"

"So did Bundy. Why else do you think he had such an easy time getting to his targets? Look, dammit, Hugh didn't kill her even though Alice fit his victim profile to a T. There's something about her that we're missing. We have to figure out what that shit is." Randall's sigh carried over the phone. "Tell me you learned something useful tonight."

Other than the damn phone call? The *two* calls that were making his stomach knot. "We've been in her place before. You searched it. You know she's not hiding anything there."

"But her guard was lowered with you. Did she say anything about Collins? Did you push her?"

Zander could see the faint lights from her cabin. "She's still freaked because the victims looked like her. When she told me that, I could see guilt on her face. Like she blamed herself because they died."

"Or...maybe she felt guilty because she *was* in on their deaths."

The guy had her tried and convicted in his mind. "I don't like the phone calls." Zander glared into the night. "You're sure they came from the same burner phone?" Julianna's parents had received one call right after their daughter had been taken. A robotic voice had told them that the caller "admired" their daughter. And then...five days later, another call had come through for the desperate parents. This time, the caller had told them where to find the body. The distorted voice had given them directions, then simply said, "She wasn't perfect."

And when the Feds had found Julianna's remains, no, she hadn't been perfect any longer — because the bastard who'd hurt her had tortured her before he'd put his knife in her heart.

"We're sure it was the same phone. The same person who called your precious Alice tonight also called Julianna's parents."

When Alice had received her calls, *Unknown Caller* had appeared on her phone's screen. But, just because that phrase had appeared, it sure as shit didn't mean you couldn't figure out who the hell had just called. Especially when you were the FBI.

"Zander." Frustration beat in Randall's voice. "Alice May has *never* been a target before."

"She wasn't a target to Hugh. But Hugh is lying in a cemetery outside of Savannah. This guy hunting now — this copycat —" *His* suspicion. Zander thought they were looking for some wannabe who'd gotten confidential information about the case — information that hadn't been given to the Press. *Like the fact that rose petals were sprinkled around the dead bodies.* That bit had never been released. The killer had carefully arranged red rose petals around his victims. Rose petals just like the ones that had been found at the church where Alice had planned to marry Hugh Collins. "If we are dealing with a copycat, then wouldn't the guy's ultimate prize be Alice? I mean, hell, killing her could be like paying homage to Hugh." Zander had seen plenty of twisted shit like that during his time in the FBI's violent crimes division. Folks got fixated on killers. They wanted to emulate them. To be them.

Thunder rumbled.

"You've got eyes on her place, right?" Zander pushed. He couldn't stand the idea of Alice being in her cabin, all alone. Not if some freak was targeting her. Not if she was —

"Oh, we've got eyes on her…"

The rain had started to fall. It came down in quick, hard torrents.

"And she's on the move."

"What?"

"Your Ms. Innocent left her cabin, in the rain, in the middle of the night, and she's running toward your place. Yeah, that screams I'm-Not-Hiding anything to me. What about you?"

What in the hell? "I'll call you back." He slammed down the phone. He could hear the rain pounding into his roof. Why would Alice be running around in the storm? He bounded toward the door. He hurried outside as thunder boomed overhead.

His gaze scanned the darkness. It took fifteen minutes to walk to her place. If she was running, she'd cut that time in half. How long ago had she left her cabin? He hadn't asked Randall. And shit, if he was just standing outside of his place, wouldn't that look suspicious to her? He should go back in his cabin. Wait and see if she came to him.

What if she isn't coming to me, though? What if she's going into the woods to meet someone else? A…partner?

He had to check this out. But he hadn't grabbed his flashlight. Or his gun. He whirled back for his cabin and rushed inside. The door slammed behind him. He got the flashlight and —

A knock sounded at his door. Zander stiffened. Then he was jerking open that door as fast as he could. Lightning lit up the sky.

Alice stood on his narrow porch. Soaking wet, with raindrops sliding off her coat. Her wet hair clung to her cheeks, and she stared up at him with eyes he'd *never* be able to forget, not in a thousand years.

"Alice? What are you doing?" Zander pulled her inside. "You shouldn't be out in this storm. You shouldn't —"

She wrapped her arms around his shoulders. Stood on her tip-toes. And kissed him. She tasted sweeter than the wine they'd had that night. She tasted like the rain. She tasted like fucking heaven.

He should back away from her. He should absolutely *not* kiss her like a starving man. He should not pull her closer, pressing his overeager dick against her.

"I want you," Alice whispered.

Damn. He was in trouble.

"I thought about you after you left…about how I haven't felt this way in a long time." She eased back a few inches, and she stared up at him. "Do you ever feel afraid, Zander?"

He didn't know what to say. His gaze had fallen to her mouth, and he was trying to figure out what to —

"Because I spend most of my days trying not to be afraid. And then you came along. When I'm with you, everything seems different."

It was different because he was lying to her.

"Don't give up on me."

He blinked. His stare locked with hers. "I wasn't planning —"

"That's what I ran through the storm to tell you." Her smile flashed, and it lit her eyes. "I wasn't always this crazy woman who barely leaves her house. I wasn't this woman who is afraid of her own shadow. I used to be so much more, and I'm trying — trying really hard — to be her again."

His chest ached. "Alice…"

"I like you. You're funny and you're smart, and you bring me cupcakes." She stood on her toes once more and kissed him. Alice gave a delighted laugh. "I've missed this. So much. Missed wanting someone. Missed just being normal." Alice shook her head. "And I probably sound like an absolutely deranged person to you right now." Red stained her cheeks as she retreated a few, quick steps. "I —"

He wasn't letting her go. She didn't sound deranged. She sounded strong. Resilient. Sexy as fuck. He stalked forward as she retreated, and he caged her between his body and the hard wood wall. "You're not leaving."

Her breath hitched.

"The storm is too bad. I can't let you go back out in it." He swallowed and grabbed his control with both hands. "You're staying here tonight."

Her eyes widened. "It's not—"

The lights went out even as more thunder boomed.

"Sweetheart," Zander said in the darkness as he inhaled her delicate scent, "there's no way you're leaving me tonight."

CHAPTER THREE

She'd acted on impulse. Mad, crazy impulse. And she'd run to see Zander. She'd been in her home, the storm had been coming...and she'd needed to see him one more time.

It felt as if she'd been sleeping for the last twelve months. Then finally, *finally,* she'd woken up.

Tomorrow was the one-year anniversary of Hugh's death. Actually...it *was* the anniversary. Midnight had already come. It *was* tomorrow.

Alice hadn't been able to stand being alone in her cabin as she stared at the clock. She'd run to Zander. To the man who had been there for her, over and over again during the last two months. Her friend.

Her...lover?

Maybe. Who knew what could—

"You're taking my bed."

Her head snapped up at his low, deep voice. Alice knew she wasn't exactly thinking clearly. Or acting clearly. The fact that it was the anniversary of her wedding day, of Hugh's death...yeah, she was a hot mess.

One thing was certain, though — she wasn't going to hide from the things she wanted any longer.

And she wanted Zander.

He stood about three feet in front of her, a determined look on his handsome face, his arms crossed over his chest. She'd ditched her rain coat — after leaving a dripping trail across his wooden floor. Despite wearing the rain coat, her t-shirt was soaked, and her wet jeans clung tightly to her. She'd already taken off her squeaky tennis shoes and her socks. She'd left them near his front door. The power had been off for about ten minutes. Zander had grabbed a flashlight, and he'd been reaching for candles — but then the lights had flashed back on in his cabin.

"You can dry off in my bathroom upstairs. I have a t-shirt you can wear." His gaze had darted down her body, but he suddenly whipped his stare up — and away from her. "And you can sleep in my bed."

She wasn't the type of woman to try and seduce a man on the first date. And it *had* been their first date. But then again, she also wasn't the type of woman to fall for a serial killer so...

Hello. Been there. Done that.

So maybe it was time to start something new. Time to be someone new. "Where will you sleep?"

"The couch."

Her stare darted to said couch. It hardly looked big enough to hold his long frame. "I don't want to kick you out of your bed." She focused on him again. "I can go back to my place."

"Hell, no. Not in this weather."

Alice shrugged and tucked a lock of wet hair behind her ear. "Then I can take the couch."

His fierce expression softened a little bit. "Sweetheart, my mother raised me to be a gentleman. No way will a lady ever sleep on a lumpy couch while my ass is spread out on a king-sized bed."

"Well, if it's king-sized, then there should be enough room for us both." There. She'd said it. She'd just put that out right in the open.

She waited.

The air itself seemed to get very, very heavy.

"You want to run that by me again?" His hands fell to his sides and fisted.

"I think there is room for us both in the bed."

"You should dry off. Get changed. Go to bed. It's late, and you don't know what the hell you're saying—"

She took her time as she eliminated the distance between them. Alice would like to think that she did a sexy stroll toward Zander, but in reality, she probably looked like a dripping wet mess. *Maybe that's why he's not jumping at the chance for sexy times with me.* She stopped right in front of him. "I know exactly what I'm saying. I know exactly what I'm doing."

A furrow appeared between his dark brows. "It took me two months to convince you to have dinner with me. Now you're ready for — "

"More than dinner," Alice finished, and she hoped he didn't realize just how hard it was to say those words. How hard it had been to go to his cabin. But she wasn't going to be the scared victim any longer. A year was long enough. "I want you. And judging by the way you kissed me, I think you want me, too."

"I'd have to be insane not to want you." His words were a rough growl.

She smiled at him. He didn't get that her self-esteem had been crap for months. That she doubted every move she made. To have someone now stare at her like she was the best thing he'd ever seen... "Thank you."

"What changed?" His hands were still fisted.

A shiver slid over her. Mostly due to the cold...or, perhaps it was due to the intense, hot look in his eyes. "I couldn't stop thinking about you after you left. And I realized I didn't want to be the same woman any longer." The woman who didn't take chances. The woman who would never think about making love with a man on the first date.

Too risky... *You don't know him well enough. You can't trust him.*

She would have bet her life on Hugh being a good man. On being someone she could trust. She would have lost her bet *and* her life.

Alice stared straight into Zander's eyes. Such dark eyes. "I want to be with you tonight. If you don't want me...if you don't want this, it's okay." She kept her chin up. "I'll go shower." A warm shower would chase away the chill from the rain. "And you can decide what you want."

He pointed to the stairs. His gaze positively burned. "The shower is at the top of the stairs."

Her body brushed against his. Was that seductive? Or clumsy? She was so out of practice at this. "Thank you."

She took her time heading to the bathroom. Trying for a sensual walk again, but probably just getting more water on his floor and stairs. Once she was inside the bathroom, Alice shut the door behind her with a soft click. Her gaze darted to the mirror.

What in the hell are you doing?

***

What in the hell was he doing? Zander caught himself before he bounded toward the bathroom. His dick was rock-hard in his jeans, shoving so tightly against the zipper that he was pretty sure he'd have an imprint on his cock. Tension tightened every muscle in his body, and he just wanted to head toward the bathroom, throw open that door—

And have her.

He closed his eyes. Counted to ten. Then fucking twenty. The lust didn't lessen. He'd known the desire he felt for Alice would be a problem. From the very first day when he'd gone to her cabin, rapped on the door, and then found himself staring into her unforgettable eyes.

Fucking problem.

But he'd thought he could hold himself in check. He'd sure as hell never expected Alice's offer...

There is room for us both in the bed.

His phone rang. The distinctive peal— metallic and flat—told him the caller was Randall. Swearing, Zander turned away from the bathroom and the roar of the shower that he could now hear. If he was going to talk to his partner, this was the time. While she was in the shower, Alice wouldn't be able to overhear his conversation.

He grabbed the phone and slipped into the kitchen. "What?" His voice was low and angry, but Zander couldn't help it.

"The weather is so freaking bad that I'm pulling the other agents back. Keep Alice May at your place for the night. We need to make sure she doesn't try to slip past our guard."

Oh, she's about to slip right under my guard, all right.

"Z?"

"What?"

"You got everything under control there?"

Not even close. "She won't leave tonight. Don't worry about it."

"Is she close by? Can she hear you?"

His hold tightened on the phone. "What the hell do you think I am? An amateur? She's in the shower. I'm going to give her dry clothes to wear, and then I'm tucking her into bed for the night."

Silence.

"Uh, *tucking* her in?" Randall coughed. "Then…you're *sure* things are under control?"

"I've got her." Why did his words come out with a hard, possessive edge?

"This could be an opportunity. Talk to her. Gain her trust—"

"I have her fucking trust." She'd come to him. Offered herself to him. And he felt like the worst kind of bastard. *Because I am.* "And everything I've learned is telling me she's innocent. Alice wasn't involved in Julianna's murder. I don't think she was involved with *any* of the kills."

"The phone calls tonight—"

"Someone is fucking with her." Zander didn't like that. Not one bit. "Instead of looking at her as the top suspect, we need to reassess. She could need our protection."

"Z—"

The shower had shut off. "I have to go. She's coming out of the shower, and I need to give her one of my t-shirts to wear."

"Z." Worry blasted in Randall's voice. "You're not sleeping with her."

It wasn't a question. And since it wasn't a question, Zander didn't give his partner an answer. He ended the call, tossed the phone onto the counter, and hurried to his bedroom. He found an old Army shirt and rushed back to the bathroom. He opened the door and slipped the shirt inside, putting it on the sink. "This is for you." The words were gruff and hard, and steam drifted out of the bathroom. He backed away, as fast as he could.

A few moments later, Alice crept out of the bathroom. "I, um, hung my wet clothes over your shower rod. Is that okay?"

She wasn't supposed to look that sexy in his shirt. He'd gotten the biggest shirt he could find, thinking it would conceal her. But...the neck of the t-shirt slipped over one of her shoulders, a sexy little slip. And the bottom of the t-shirt fell to mid-thigh on her. Alice had incredible legs.

The fabric of the shirt was old and worn, and he could easily see the thrust of her tight nipples against—

"Is that okay?" Alice repeated.

He spun on his heel, giving her his back. "Absolutely." A snap.

"Zander?"

"You're sleeping in the bedroom." He was *trying* to keep his control. Trying really hard not to pounce on her. FBI agents didn't pounce. "I'm on the couch."

"You...you don't want me."

He sucked in a deep breath and slowly turned toward her. "I can't remember wanting a woman this much." And that wasn't some line. Not some BS that he threw out to make her feel more connected to him. It was the absolute truth. "But you need to be *sure.* Sure of yourself. Sure of me. Before we take a step that we can't take back." Every time he pulled in a breath, Zander swore he tasted her. "If I have you, I don't think I'd be able to let go."

Wait. Where in the hell had those words just come from?

But...he meant them. Something told him this wouldn't be a one-time deal, not for him, and not for her. And he *knew* how important this particular date was for Alice. There was no way he could have worked the Secret Admirer case and not understood the importance of this particular first anniversary.

Alice had come to him just after midnight. She'd come to him on the one-year anniversary of Hugh's death. On the anniversary of the date her life had gone to hell.

He was *trying* to do the right thing, a hard feat when every part of him wanted to do so many very, very wrong things to her. With her. In that big bed just waiting in the bedroom... "See if you still feel the same way in the daylight," he rasped. *See if you still feel the same way when demons aren't chasing you.*

Alice's eyes were so big and deep. She stared at him a moment longer, then, without a word, she padded into the bedroom. Zander didn't realize he was holding his breath, not until the door closed softly behind her.

When it did...

He exhaled. Shuddered.

Then he marched into the bathroom and prepared for one very cold shower.

***

Her cabin was dark and still. Rain pounded down, and thunder rumbled, hiding his approach. He'd planned this moment for so long. It was finally *his* time.

Getting inside was easy. Her locks were a joke, and Alice hadn't remembered to turn on her security system. She'd always been far too trusting.

So many days — weeks — had passed since he'd last seen her in person. Had she missed him? He'd certainly missed her. He climbed up the stairs. The third stair creaked, but the soft sound was swallowed by the storm's fury. Up, up he went, and then he was at the top of the stairs. A door waited to his right. Alice's bedroom.

He opened the door. The hinges didn't squeak, there was no sound at all, and then he was inside. Rain drops fell off him, trailing onto the floor as he approached the bed.

Lightning flashed, illuminating the room.

Illuminating the empty bed.

He stopped cold a moment, shock rolling through him. Where in the hell was Alice? It was *their* day. She should have been in the bed. She should have been waiting for him.

He bent, and his hand went to the knife that he kept strapped inside his boot. The knife that he *hadn't* intended to use on Alice. Not on his Alice.

But…rage grew inside of him.

It twisted. It surged. It consumed.

Alice wasn't there.

He slashed the knife into her pillow. Into her bed. He cut through her sheets and her covers.

Alice wasn't *there.*
So where in the hell was she?

CHAPTER FOUR

Her scream sent adrenaline coursing through Zander's body. He jerked upright and nearly tumbled off the narrow couch. Lightning flashed, illuminating the den, even as his frantic gaze went to the nearby clock on the wall. Three a.m. He hadn't been sleeping, he'd been fucking thinking about her —

Another scream came, and Zander leapt off the couch. His heart thundered in his chest as he ran for the bedroom. When he reached the door, he kicked it in, not even hesitating. "Alice!" He hit the lights.

She shot upright and her wide eyes immediately locked on him. Her chest heaved, rising far too quickly as she drew in desperate gulps of air.

"What's happening? What's wrong?" His stare shot around the room, but he didn't see any sign of a threat. Zander stalked closer to her.

"I'm sorry." Her hair had dried, and it slid over her shoulders. "I had a-a bad dream. I didn't mean to wake you up."

He found himself sitting on the edge of the bed. His hand lifted, and he brushed back a heavy lock of her hair, tucking it behind her left ear. "You have a lot of bad dreams?"

Alice gave a slow nod. "Unfortunately."

"Want to talk about it?"

Her gaze slid away from him. "In the dream..." She swallowed. "I was one of Hugh's victims. He had me tied down, and he was coming toward me with a knife."

Shit. "Baby..."

She reached for him, moving fast, and suddenly, Alice's hands were around his shoulders, and her mouth was pressed against his. She kissed him with a desperation, a wild need, and Zander's response was instant.

Desire ignited. Lust burned. He'd tried to fight his attraction to her. Tried to just do the damn job. But it was three a.m. She was kissing him. She wanted him.

And he wasn't going to be able to pull away. Not this time.

"I could have been another victim. I could have died." Her words tumbled out as she eased away a few inches. "I want to live."

She was alive. She was —

Her hands moved to his chest. He wasn't wearing a shirt. Before he'd crashed onto the couch, he'd stripped down so that he only wore his boxers, and they weren't exactly providing him with a lot of coverage. Her silken fingers trailed over his chest, and her tongue slid along his lower lip.

"I want you," Alice whispered.

He felt his control shatter. Zander tumbled her back onto the bed. And he let his desire loose. His kiss was demanding and ravenous. His hands snaked along her body. Slid under the edge of the shirt she wore—*his* shirt—and he touched smooth, perfect skin.

She moaned into his mouth, and he absolutely loved that husky sound. He wanted to hear more moans. Wanted to drive her wild. He was beyond rational thought. All he knew was need.

A need that threatened to swallow them both whole.

He got the t-shirt off her. Threw it somewhere. Then Zander was kissing a path down her neck and finding her sensitive spots. Memorizing them. Licking and kissing and even lightly biting as he marked her. Down he went. Her breasts thrust toward him, the nipples light and dusky, and he had to take one into his mouth. Had to suck and make her moan again. He treated the other breast to the same sensual attention. Her hips jerked up against him, moving in a fast rhythm against his cock.

Her legs were spread. He was already positioned between them. His cock—covered

only by the boxers — shoved toward her sex.
Sinking into her would feel like paradise, he
knew it.

But she had to be ready. Had to be as wild as
he was.

His fingers caressed over her abdomen. Her
nails bit into his shoulders. He eased his hand
down more, moved it between their bodies.
Stroked her very core.

She was wet for him. Hot. And when he
pushed one finger into her, then another...

"*Zander!*" Fierce need had her crying out his
name.

He felt as if he'd erupt at any moment. He
had to get inside her. Right the hell then.

But...

He wanted to taste her. Wanted to make her
come. Wanted her to go insane for him.

He slid down her body. Spread her thighs
even wider, and he put his mouth on her. She
stiffened, then arched toward him, moaning
eagerly when his tongue went to work. Licking,
stroking, and tasting heaven, Zander feasted.

She came against his mouth. The release
rocked through her whole body, and he loved the
way she cried out his name. No inhibition. No
hiding. Just pleasure.

He licked her again, then pulled away long
enough to fumble for the nightstand. He yanked
out a condom from the box there and had it on

seconds later. Then he was pushing his eager cock toward the entrance of her body. Locking his fingers with hers. Driving in—

So tight.

She stiffened beneath him, and Zander cursed himself. He was being too rough with her. He needed to ease up, to—

"It's...been a while," she gasped.

His fingers slid back to her clit. He stroked her. Didn't move his cock an inch forward. He wouldn't, not until she was ready.

She relaxed around him as he strummed her clit. As he caressed her, Alice gave the moan he was becoming greedy to hear. Then her legs lifted and locked around his hips. She was the one to move. The one to arch up against him and take his cock in deep.

And when he was balls deep into her, Zander nearly lost his mind. Hot. Wet. *So tight.* He withdrew, thrust deep, over and over, as the rhythm became wilder. She was with him every second, driving for the release of pleasure, for the avalanche that would come. The slap of their bodies filled the air, the scent of sex, the sound of their panting breaths and then...Alice jerked beneath him. She gave a little scream, and he felt the fierce contractions of her release around his cock. Zander followed her into oblivion.

***

When she woke up again, Alice wasn't alone.
A warm, strong arm had curled around her
stomach, and her body was tucked in close to
Zander.

They'd had incredible sex. The best sex she'd
ever had. Then he'd held her while she slept.
She'd dreaded the anniversary of Hugh's death.
Dreaded waking up to his ghost, but she wasn't
staring at a twisted past.

She was staring at Zander's handsome face.
When he slept, his features softened a bit. Sure,
his jaw was still as hard, but his lips had curved
into what looked like a faint smile. His long
lashes — thick and dark — shielded his intense
gaze. A line of stubble covered his jaw, and she
found herself leaning forward and pressing a
quick kiss to his cheek.

"Good morning, sweetheart," he murmured.

She realized he'd been awake. Then she
wondered — just how long *had* he been awake?

His eyes opened. No sleepiness there.
Absolute awareness. His faint smile deepened.
"Sleep well?"

After the mind-blowing sex? Yes, she
absolutely had. No more bad dreams. No
nightmares that left her screaming, thank you
very much. Alice gave a quick nod as she sat up
and pulled the covers with her. She needed the
covers because Alice had just realized she was

completely naked. She hadn't cared last night. But this morning, she felt shy.

Probably because she hadn't done the morning-after routine in a very, very long time.

His fingers rose and trailed over her suddenly hot cheeks. "What's the cute blush about?"

"It's…" *Be honest.* "It's about me not knowing what I should say to you right now."

His eyes narrowed. Zander seemed to mull something over in his head, and then he finally said, "Last night, you mentioned that it had been a long time for you."

She knew her blush had to be getting deeper. There was no way she could play this situation off casually. "It had been a while." Oh, jeez, she'd thought he'd enjoyed himself. Maybe he hadn't experienced the insane pleasure that she'd had. Maybe —

"How long?"

She wanted to hunch her shoulders and hide under the covers. Because she wanted that, Alice lifted her chin and squared her shoulders. "Since Hugh."

A muscle flexed in his jaw. "You haven't been with anyone since the Secret Admirer?"

She flinched. Alice couldn't help it. She tried to think of him as Hugh. If she thought of him as just Hugh, then she could almost pretend the

Secret Admirer had been someone different. A monster she hadn't met. A monster —

I didn't have in my bed.

But lying wasn't going to help her. "I haven't been with anyone since the Secret Admirer." There. She'd said it. Chill bumps rose on her body. "So, um, if I was...um..." God. Her cheeks were *burning*. "If things weren't good enough — " She started to slip from the bed.

But Zander yanked her back. He tumbled her onto the mattress and leaned over her, staring down at her with glittering eyes. "The sex was more than good enough. It was fucking mind blowing."

Wait — it had been? Her lips curled. "I...thought so, too."

"*You* are good enough. Never doubt that, Alice. Never. Do you hear me?"

She swallowed. "I hear you." His voice had been nearly booming. It would have been hard *not* to hear him.

Zander pressed a hard kiss to her lips. "Glad we got that cleared up." Then his head lifted, and he stared at her as if he were trying to figure out some puzzle. "Why in the hell did you pick me?"

"Pick you?"

"To have sex with, baby. You're fucking gorgeous. I'm sure there have been guys fighting to be with you." He caged her with his body.

She caught her lower lip between her teeth as she thought this through. Oh, hell, why hesitate? *Just be honest.* "After the news broke, there were plenty of men who were interested in me. Turns out, there's a whole group of guys out there who are fascinated by killers. And getting to fuck the ex-fiancée of the Secret Admirer?" She had to swallow twice in order to get the lump out of her throat. "Well, that to-do item was suddenly on the minds of those men."

He swore.

"Yes, exactly." She eased out a breath. "You know how there are those women who want to have sex with killers? The ones who want to marry them? There are plenty of men who want that same, dangerous thrill. They thought that by being close to me, they'd get that rush."

"You told them all to fuck off." His gaze blazed.

"I absolutely did. Some didn't take the news too easily."

A line appeared between his brows. "What happened?" An angry growl.

"A few break-ins at my place. Some underwear was stolen. Things that creeped me the hell out." Her tongue swiped over her lower lip. "All signs that told me I needed to get out of that town and start over some place new."

His fingers brushed over her cheek in a tender caress. "You still didn't say why you chose me."

"There were some other guys who didn't seem like total freaks." Not that she had good radar for determining that, obviously, seeing as how she'd almost married a serial killer but... "I wasn't exactly looking to join the dating game at that time."

"And you are now?"

"I honestly have no idea what I'm looking for right now. I just know..." She couldn't seem to find the right words to make him understand. "You were different. You *are* different. You've been there every time I needed you. And you...you didn't give up on me."

He pressed another kiss to her lips. "I won't ever give up."

She didn't feel cold. No chills. His words had warmth spreading through her.

"I'm going to make you breakfast." Another kiss from him. This one was slower, though. More sensual. "I think I've got some cinnamon rolls in there. Should be perfect for your sweet tooth."

She gave a little laugh. It was crazy. She was in bed with a lover, laughing, acting so normal. This was what she'd been missing for the last year. *No, Zander is what I've been missing.*

He slid from the bed, giving her a stellar view of his tight ass. She whistled, and he glanced back, smiling at her.

The man had a killer smile.

***

As soon as he left the bedroom, Zander's smile vanished. He'd palmed his phone before he exited the room, and he glanced down, seeing the line of missed texts. All from Randall. Shit. Zander called his partner and put the phone to his ear as he hurried into the kitchen. Randall answered on the second ring. "What the hell, man?" Zander demanded before Randall could even say hello. "*Seven* missed texts?"

"Glad you're still alive," Randall snapped.

Zander fired a quick look over his shoulder. "Don't start this shit with me. I kept her in the house, just like you ordered."

"And did you keep your hands off her?"

He pitched his voice low as he snarled, "The profilers have been wrong about her. She's not like you think. Not like *they* think."

"Dammit. You fucked her."

"Randall, you don't understand her. Alice isn't cold and calculating. She's—"

"You're talking like a blind, lovesick fool, Z."

"I'm not blind. I'm telling you—she's not like you think." She hadn't even been with a lover since Hugh. *Not until me.* She was scared and shy, and when she looked at him — fuck, he felt like a bastard.

"Have you considered that maybe she's just a good liar?"

Yeah, he had considered that shit. Especially since Zander happened to be a good liar, himself.

"Question her. If you fucked her, shit, at least use that to our advantage. If she's seems to trust you, grill her. This is your chance." Randall hung up.

Sonofabitch.

Zander slammed the phone down on the kitchen table. He'd always wanted to be an FBI agent. Wanted to make a difference. But right then, he damn well hated the job.

CHAPTER FIVE

Alice's tongue swiped over her lower lip as she licked away a trace of cinnamon icing. Zander's whole body tensed, and he tried not to think about all of the things he wanted her to do with her sexy little tongue.

"Breakfast was delicious. Thank you. No one has made breakfast for me in a very long time." She flashed him a wide smile. He loved her smiles. She'd smiled a lot that morning, and every time her lips curled, his chest seemed to ache. "But, um," Alice glanced at the clock, "I think I'd better be going home. I need to make sure there wasn't any damage from the storm."

"I'll walk you over."

Her smile stretched a little more. Her eyes seemed to gleam. "Thank you."

Hell. She was looking at him like he was some kind of white knight. She didn't realize he was the lying asshole who'd been sabotaging her life. She helped him clean up in the kitchen, and a few moments later, they were walking through the woods. The air was crisp, a little cool, but the sky was a bright blue overhead.

He took her hand and threaded his fingers with hers. Her hand was so much smaller than his, but it oddly seemed to fit perfectly against his.

"The calm after the storm," Alice murmured as she glanced up the sky. "Always my favorite part."

He kept pace with her, moving slowly, and then… "Mind if I ask you a question?"

"Go ahead." Another smile from her. But the gleam in her eyes had dimmed.

"You really didn't know? I mean, about your ex. You didn't know the guy was —"

She stopped walking. The sunlight fell down on her. "I didn't know Hugh was a killer. I had no idea that the man in my bed, the man I was going to marry, had been torturing and murdering women." Now her smile was gone. "If I'd known, I would have stopped him. I would have gone to the police. I would have tried to *help* those victims." Her chin lifted. "He'd just killed the last one the night before, did you know that? If I'd just realized what was happening…I could have saved her. Her dead body was —" But she broke off, shaking her head.

She'd turned pale in the sunlight. He was a total bastard, and he pushed her as he said, "Photos were found at your place."

Alice took a step back. She pulled her hand from his. "I didn't know they were there. Hugh must have hidden them under the floor. I…I went to a shrink once. I was so scared, all the time, and he told me—the shrink said Hugh had probably put them there because he wanted to relive his crimes. He liked having the photos close to me. Since I looked so much like the victims, Hugh could think about the crime photos, he could think about me and—"

Fucking sonofabitch. A tear had just slid down her cheek. "Stop." Zander knew this theory. It had been floated around at the FBI office, too.

Victim or killer. The eternal debate when it came to Alice May.

Her breath came a little too fast.

"Why'd you only go see the shrink once?" A softer question, and he watched her carefully.

"Because by the end of the session, I realized he was talking more about Hugh than me. Everything came back to Hugh. The shrink—I swear, *he* was obsessed with killers. He thought there was something about *me* that had drawn Hugh and I together. That I was just as twisted inside."

Zander swore. "He told you that shit?"

"No, he used much nicer words. But he really was looking forward to, um, I think he said, 'unraveling the darkness of my mind' during our sessions." She shook her head. "Baring my soul to strangers isn't high on my to-do list. Just talking about this to you is kind of taking all the courage that I have."

His eyes widened. "Then why are you telling me?"

"Because I think you matter. And I don't want to screw this up by keeping secrets." She squared her delicate shoulders. "I didn't know. I never participated in anything he did. And if I could go back, *I'd* stop the Secret Admirer."

He believed her. Randall would say he was being a blind bastard, that Zander had nothing to go on but instinct. An instinct that was screwed because Zander was letting lust get in his way. He—

Alice was walking again. He fell into step beside her.

"You'll have to tell me your secrets, too," Alice murmured.

Now he was the one to stiffen. *Baby, you'll hate my secrets.*

"Sooner or later," she added.

Later. Much fucking later. That would be the best plan. Because when Alice found out all the lies he'd told to her, she'd shut him out. As fast as she could.

And Zander didn't want to be shut out of Alice's life.

All too soon, they were back at her cabin. The place looked quiet, and the windows gleamed in the morning light. He walked Alice to the front door, and she turned toward him. "I'm sorry I crashed your place in the middle of a rainstorm."

His lips quirked. "Don't be." His hand cupped her cheek. "Come crash with me anytime."

Her gaze searched his. "You…you are a good person, right, Zander? I'm not going to find out that you've got some whole other life I don't know anything about?"

Hell. Could the knife twist in his gut any deeper? Careful with his words, he told her, "I don't break the law, baby. I haven't done anything that would ever get me arrested, but I'm not some angel."

"I don't think anyone is. I just need you to really, really not be the devil."

Because she'd almost married that particular bastard.

"I'm not the devil." He leaned forward and pressed a quick kiss to her lips. "Dinner tonight?"

She gave him the gift of her smile. "I'd like that."

"My place," he added. "I get to cook this time."

She kissed him, and her hands pressed lightly to his shirt-front. He swore he could feel her touch burn right through to his skin. His overeager dick thrust toward her, but Zander held tight to his control. He had to check in with the other agents, and those guys probably had eyes on him and Alice right then. He wasn't about to give them a fucking show.

"Six o'clock," he said against her sweet lips. "I'll see you then."

Alice pulled away. She took the keys out of her pocket, and a few moments later, she'd opened the door. Alice glanced back at him. She smiled at him once more, right before she shut the door.

He stood there a moment, her smile locked in his mind. The woman had a gorgeous smile. Everything about her was sexy as hell, and if he could just prove to the others that she wasn't guilty, then—

A scream seemed to echo in the air. *Her* scream. A scream that came from inside the cabin. Not hesitating, Zander immediately kicked in the front door. It flew back, slamming into the wall. But he was already racing inside. Another scream echoed, one filled with shock and fear, and he bounded up the stairs as he followed that sound. He turned to the right, toward *her* bedroom. "Alice!"

She whirled toward him. Her eyes were huge. Stark. Her body trembled.

His gaze swept over her. *No injury.* Thank Christ. But then his stare took in the room around her. The bedding that had been slashed. The clothes that were tossed around the room. Clothes that were also in ribbons. As if someone had taken a knife to them. Cut them. Destroyed them.

Drawers were thrown against the wall. Her dresser mirror had been smashed. Books were ripped apart. Absolute destruction.

Alice bent to pick up a shredded gown. "Who did this?"

He grabbed her hand. "Don't touch it." His voice was low and lethal.

"Zander?"

"Don't touch a damn thing. Not until I get a team in here."

"What?"

But he was already pulling her out of the room, nearly dragging her with him down the stairs. As far as he knew, the perp could still be in the house. His priority was getting her to safety. When she was safe, he'd get the house secured. His team could come in. They'd search for prints. They'd find out what in the hell had happened.

He reached the landing. She dug in her heels. "Zander, *stop!* I'm not leaving this house! I'm going back upstairs, and I'm going to—"

No damn way. He just scooped her up and put her over his shoulder.

"What in the hell are you doing?"

The front door was still open. He rushed through it and hurried toward the cover of the trees. He didn't want to present a target to anyone who might be watching. As soon as they were clear, he lowered her to the ground.

"Are you crazy?" She tried to lunge away.

He just pulled her right back against him. And he yanked out his phone. Luckily, he had a fucking signal. He called Randall, and his partner answered on the first ring. "Move the team in, *now,*" Zander barked. "Someone was in her place last night. Her bedroom has been trashed."

"What?"

"I've got her. We're outside, and she's secure. Get the agents moving. Hurry the hell up!"

"On the damn way."

Zander shoved the phone back into his pocket.

Silence.

Shit. *Shit.*

His gaze lifted. Alice was staring straight at him. She wasn't fighting to get away from him any longer. Her body was statue-still. "What men?"

He squared his shoulders. "FBI agents."

They would be there in moments.

"We can't touch the house," Zander added, making his voice flat with an effort, "not until they get here. We'll need to get a crime scene team inside. If the perp left prints — "

"You're not…not a handyman, are you?" Her eyes had never seemed bigger or deeper.

"I'm damn handy. You've seen for yourself just what I can—"

"*Don't.*" She swallowed. "Who in the hell are you?"

He could hear the thunder of footsteps already. His team was sweeping in. "My name is Zander Todd. Just like I told you." He hadn't lied about his name. But as for the rest… "And I'm FBI."

***

They hadn't let her go back in her home. As soon as the FBI agents had swarmed, she'd been escorted to a black SUV. She'd been told to get inside, and then some other agent—Randall something—had driven her to town. To the sheriff's office. They'd put her in a small, tight room, and she'd been sitting there ever since.

It's just like the day of my wedding. I was taken away. Locked in a room. And I waited and waited.

Then my whole world fell apart.

A cold cup of coffee waited in front of her. Her reflection stared back at her from the one-way mirror on the nearby wall. A clock ticked far too loudly, counting off the seconds at an excruciating pace.

Then…the door opened.

Her gaze immediately flew toward the door as she stiffened. She expected to see Zander standing there. Instead, she stared at a man with warm, mocha skin and hard, suspicious eyes. The agent she'd met before. Randall. Randall — what had been his last name? Her world had pretty much been spinning out of control when he'd introduced himself before.

When he'd introduced himself and then shoved her into the back of an SUV.

She struggled to pull up his name and — *Cane.* It had been Randall Cane.

"Thanks for waiting, Ms. May," he murmured, the faint hint of a Boston accent sliding through his words. "I have a few questions for you." He stalked toward the small table. Took the seat across from her.

She blinked at him. "I have a few questions for you, too." Her gaze darted to the one-way mirror. "Where is Zander?"

"Agent Todd is tying up a few loose ends. He'll be in soon enough."

Agent Todd. Goosebumps rose on her arms.

"What time did you leave your house last night?"

"I…midnight. Right after midnight. Like, twelve-oh-three."

He jotted down some notes and peered up at her. "That's very specific."

Why play games? He might like doing that. *Agent Todd* might enjoy games. But she didn't. "Today is kind of a special anniversary." Understatement of the century. "I was dreading this day, okay? So I was watching my clock as the time passed."

"And at twelve-oh-three, you decided to leave your house, even though the weather was shit, and head to visit Agent Todd."

"I didn't know he was an agent." She stared straight ahead and ignored the chill that snaked around her whole body. "But, yes, I decided to go visit him then."

"In the middle of the night. Twelve-oh-three." He tapped his pen against the table. "Why'd you do that?"

Her heart raced in her chest. "Because I wanted to see him." She tucked a lock of hair behind her ear.

His eyes narrowed on her. "And it couldn't wait until morning?"

He wasn't going to buy her story. Wasn't going to understand that she'd needed to act. Needed to get out of that house. Needed Zander.

Only Zander wasn't the man she'd thought. *Fool me once…*

"Ms. May?"

"No, it couldn't wait until morning."

He arched one brow.

The door opened. Softly. A creak of sound. Even before she turned her head, Alice knew...

Zander was there. He stood in the doorway, filling it with his broad shoulders and muscled build. He still wore jeans and a black t-shirt, but a badge was now clipped to his waist. His hair was tousled, as if he'd raked his fingers through the thick mess a few times. He looked rough, dangerous, and sexy.

He looked like a damn liar.

Zander rasped, "Alice..."

Her gaze whipped back to Randall. "What other questions do you have?"

His stare drifted between her and Zander. Then back to her. "When you returned to your house this morning, what did you do?"

"I went straight upstairs. I was planning to shower, but when I got to my room, I realized that—" *Fear.* She'd walked into her bedroom, and frozen with fear. The scream had seemed to echo distantly around her. Alice swallowed. "I realized that someone had been inside. Someone had destroyed my clothes. My furniture. Everything in that room."

"And who do you think did that?" Randall wanted to know.

She barely bit back... *You're the FBI agent. You tell me.* Her temples were throbbing. Her stomach in absolute knots. "It's the anniversary of Hugh's death. If I had to guess who'd done it, I'd say it was one of his crime groupies. Someone who wanted to make sure I didn't forget Hugh's twisted legacy." She focused on breathing. Nice and slow. "It's not the first time I've had my home broken into. You can check the police records in Savannah. When I lived there, I had a few break-ins."

Zander marched toward the table. The space was already small, and he made it feel even smaller. He stopped right next to her. "But you haven't experienced break-ins since you moved up here?"

She didn't want to look at him. Looking at him hurt. Obviously, the guy had been doing undercover work. She got that. And, obviously, she'd been his target.

Why? Probably because the FBI still mistakenly thought she'd been involved with Hugh's crimes. How many times did she have to tell them they were wrong?

"Alice?" Zander pushed.

She licked her lips. "No, there haven't been any break-ins here. I thought I was safe." Her shoulders rolled back. "Guess I was wrong."

Randall's sharp eyes swept over her face. "Did you see anyone when you went inside your house?"

"No. Didn't see anyone, and nothing seemed to be touched—at least, not downstairs. And I only got to see my bedroom really before I was pulled out." *By an agent. My new lover – the agent.* Shit. "So, uh, if more rooms were ransacked, I don't know—"

"It was just the bedroom," Zander cut in. "From what we can tell, the perp focused there." He paused. "There seemed to be a whole lot of rage in the attack."

She'd thought the same thing.

Randall cleared his throat. "Tell me, Ms. May, do you feel a lot of rage?"

It took a moment too long for his words to register. When they did, she leapt to her feet, sending her chair topping behind her. "What?"

But Randall nodded. "I'll take that as a yes."

No, no, this *wasn't* happening. "You think I did this? You think I destroyed my own stuff?

"That is one possibility," Randall allowed as he stroked his chin.

Her hands slapped down on the table. "It's not. I didn't do it. I—"

"You could have destroyed your room *before* you went to visit Agent Todd last night. After all, as you said, it was the anniversary of Hugh's death. Maybe you got emotional. Maybe your fury took over. Maybe you had to let the rage out. You destroyed the room, and then you went on your little trek through the woods. Perhaps you planned out a whole, dramatic scene."

"No, I—"

"You could have planned to bring Agent Todd back to your house. Maybe you were going to create a dramatic scene where you screamed, and he came rushing to your rescue."

Her heart was pounding far too fast. "I don't want anyone to rescue me."

Randall shrugged. "Then maybe you just wanted to throw the FBI off your trail. Is that what happened? You realized we were watching you."

God, how long had they been watching?

"You realized we were going to tie you to the murder of Julianna Stiles."

Who?

"And you wanted to make Agent Todd believe you were innocent. A victim. So you set the scene and —"

Her gaze snapped to Zander. "I didn't know you were FBI." That betrayal was still too fresh and painful.

"Alice —" Zander began, voice rough.

But she'd already turned her stare back on Randall. "Who is Julianna Stiles?"

"Oh, she's just the Secret Admirer's latest victim," Randall told her, waving his hand vaguely in the air.

That…wasn't possible. Hugh was dead.

But Randall had opened a manila file. *No, God, not another one of those!* The agents in Savannah had loved opening their files and making her look at crime scene photos. Must be some kind of FBI protocol shit because, sure enough, Randall proceeded to pull out some photos. He shoved them across the table at her, and Alice automatically glanced down.

A brunette woman. Heart-shaped face. A woman who looked so similar to Alice. A woman who had a knife sticking out of her chest. There were close-up shots of her body — of the slashes on her arms. On her neck. On her face.

"You just had to pick up where your lover left off, didn't you?" Now Randall had risen to his feet.

Alice backed away from the table. "I didn't — I've never hurt anyone!"

"So, what, you just watched before?" Randall hammered at her. "Watched while Hugh killed the others, but when he died, you decided to finally step it up with Julianna? Decided it was your time to — "

"No!" Alice practically screamed. *It can't be happening again.* "I never knew! And I didn't do this!" She pointed at the victim's pictures with a shaking hand.

But Randall just smiled at her. "Really?"
Yes, really!

Her legs were shaking. Her whole body was shaking. This couldn't be happening. Could. Not. Be.

She'd woken up in bed with Zander that morning. She'd been *happy*. Finally, things were turning around for her.

Then she'd seen her bedroom.

And her past had sucked her right back in.

"Alice?" Zander reached for her arm.

She flinched away from him. She could feel a tear sliding down her cheek. "You think I killed that woman?" Alice made herself stare into his eyes.

He didn't answer her.

The man who'd made love to her the night before — he thought she was a killer.

But, then, no, he hadn't made love to her. He'd fucked her. There was a difference. Right?

"I didn't hurt anyone," Alice whispered. She sucked in a deep breath and tried to hold herself together for just a little while longer. "And if you want to charge me, then do it. Otherwise, I'm walking out of this place right now."

A muscle flexed in Zander's jaw.

"You're free to go," Randall told her. "For now."

Alice could only shake her head. She rushed toward the door, making sure that she didn't touch Zander on her way out. She felt like her body might shatter into a million pieces. She needed to get out of that station. Needed to get some fresh air. To breathe.

But—

"Alice, stop!"

A hard hand closed over her shoulder. She was pulled back, and Alice whipped around to find Zander staring down at her.

"Get your hand off me," she ordered. "Right now."

His hand fell away.

They were in the lobby of the sheriff's station. People were watching them. Straining to listen. Uniformed deputies. FBI agents.

"You lied to me," Alice said, her voice thick with anger and pain.

"I was doing my *job*."

That jab went straight to her heart. "That's what you were doing last night?"

He flinched. "Alice—"

"I didn't hurt that woman. I never hurt *any* of them." She wouldn't break down in front of him and all of the others there. She'd get out of this place. She'd walk back to her cabin if she had to do it. "Stay away from me, understand?"

But Zander shook his head. "That's not going to be possible. We have to investigate the break-in at your cabin."

"Get another agent to do it. I want you far away from me." Because he'd hurt her, damn him. She'd opened up and trusted someone.

Only to find herself betrayed...*again*.

She spun away and rushed out of the station's glass front door. The sun glared down on her as Alice hurried down the stone steps. She didn't look back, not even when she heard the door opening behind her. She knew it was Zander. Knew that he'd followed her. She ran toward the road. She'd get out of there. She'd—

A car's engine growled. Alice's head whipped up, just in time to see a dark sedan surging toward her. Time seemed to slow down. She couldn't look past the front of that car, the gleaming bumper headed straight toward her.

But then something else hit her. *Someone.* She was wrapped in strong arms, and Alice found herself hurtling across the road. The sedan flew by her, missing her body by inches, and Alice struggled to suck in a deep breath.

"Are you okay?"

Zander's voice. Zander was right above her. He'd grabbed her. Shoved her out of the sedan's path, and they'd both hit the pavement far too hard.

"Baby?" His hands were tight on her. "Are you okay?"

"Y-yes…"

He pulled Alice to her feet. The sedan was long gone. "The sonofabitch never even braked. And I swear, it looked like he was fucking *aiming* at you."

Deputies and FBI agents were spilling out of the station and rushing toward them.

"I got the tag," Zander called out to them. He was still holding her hand. Still keeping her close. His voice lowered as he said, "We're going to get the jerk, don't worry."

But she was worried. No, she was actually scared to death.

Because someone had broken into her home. Destroyed her bedroom.

And now…

She'd almost been killed.

Alice was pretty sure the day couldn't get much worse.

CHAPTER SIX

The deputies found the black sedan — it was a stolen ride that had been abandoned at the edge of town. There was no sign of the driver, and as he stared at the vehicle, Zander knew things were only going to get worse.

"A hit and run," he muttered as Randall came to his side. "Right in front of the sheriff's station. That sure as hell takes a lot of balls."

Randall swiped a hand over his jaw. "Technically, there wasn't a hit."

Only because Zander had been able to get Alice out of the way in time. "He aimed for her." And that shit had his hands clenching. "He switched lanes just to hit her. The driver wanted to hurt Alice."

Randall's head turned, and he met Zander's stare. "We both know there are a lot of people out there who think Alice needs to pay, Z."

The families of the victims were right at the top of that list. They'd raged at the FBI offices. Pressed prosecutors. Demanded justice. But there just hadn't been enough evidence to link Alice to the Secret Admirer's crimes.

And Zander thought it was because...*she's not guilty.*

"The one-year anniversary," Zander muttered. "And things are going to hell."

"You can say that again." Randall gave a grim nod.

"Agents!" A young deputy's voice cracked with excitement. "We've got something!"

They immediately raced toward the sedan just as a crime scene tech lifted a necklace out of the vehicle. Her gloved fingers trembled a bit around the evidence. "It was inside the glove compartment." She lifted it higher, and Zander could see the face of the pendant. It was engraved with a cursive J.

His shoulders tensed. He'd seen that necklace before. "With all of my love, Mark."

Randall swore, obviously making the connection, too.

But the deputy and the tech just frowned at Zander.

"Check the back," he ordered flatly. "See if that inscription is there. *With all of my love, Mark.*"

The tech turned the necklace over. Her eyes widened. "How did you know?"

"I know," Zander explained as his heart raced faster, "because that necklace belongs to a woman who was murdered. Julianna Stiles. Her boyfriend gave her that necklace, and it hadn't been seen since the night she was abducted." Abducted, tortured, then killed — in the exact same manner as the other victims of the Secret Admirer. "Fucking hell."

"Bag it," Randall ordered the tech. "And make sure you go over every single inch of this car." He grabbed Zander's elbow and pushed him back from the scene. "Sonofabitch. You know what this means?"

Of course, he fucking knew. "He left that necklace in the car deliberately. He wanted us to know what he'd done. Who he was."

What he'd done...*murdered Julianna Stiles.*

Who he was...*the damn killer.*

"You didn't get a look at the driver? Didn't see anything about him?"

If only. "I just saw Alice. I was focused on getting to her." Once he'd had her out of the road, he'd glanced back in time to see the license plate. But no, he'd never gotten a look at the driver. Alice had already told him that she hadn't been able to see the fellow, either.

Zander released a slow breath. "He aimed for Alice."

Randall's eyes had gone wide. "She's his target. The break-in...shit, he went there for her. But she was with you last night. Then we took her to the station, and he still followed. He's after Alice."

Zander's whole body tensed.

"He'll come for her again," Randall said.

"The Secret Admirer never tried to hit someone with his car." Didn't make a bit of sense. Unless… "Shit, he wanted to separate her from us. We were in his way." And now, Alice was at the hospital. She'd been sent over in an ambulance after the attack, just as a precaution. A precaution that Zander had insisted upon. He'd also made sure a deputy accompanied her. That deputy had better be sticking to her like glue.

He spun to head back to his vehicle.

Randall grabbed his arm. "If she's really the target—"

If? Her bedroom had been destroyed. She'd been inches away from getting hit by the sedan.

"If she's the target, then we can use her, Z."

Zander stiffened as he studied at his friend.

"She can draw him in. We can catch the sonofabitch." Randall nodded decisively, as if he'd just come up with the best plan ever.

"You want her to be bait for a killer?" Fuck that shit. *Worst* plan ever.

"You told me that Alice said she wished she could have stopped the killer before he hurt those other women."

"Yeah? So?"

"This is her chance to stop him."

It was also her chance to die. From what they'd seen and learned, Hugh Collins had never intended to kill Alice. He'd loved her, as much as he *could* love. But this perp — this perp was different.

This perp wanted Alice to die.

***

A knock sounded at her hospital room door.

Alice looked up, hating that she was in that place with its white walls and sterile smells. After arriving, a nurse had instructed Alice to put on a hospital gown, and she'd been given a room. Then Alice had been poked and prodded by a young doctor — a doctor who had asked her to stay the night for observation. Why? As far as Alice was concerned, she was absolutely fine. A few scrapes and some bruises, but nothing that wouldn't heal.

"I have a delivery for you." A woman with dark hair gave Alice a wide smile. She stood just inside the hospital room. Alice hadn't even heard her enter. "An order came in through our online system. Someone wanted you to get better soon." She held a vase full of red roses in her hands.

Alice stiffened at the sight of those roses.

She'd hated roses, ever since her wedding day.

Hated them even more when she'd learned that the Secret Admirer had sent roses to the victims he'd stalked.

"I'll put them beside the bed." The woman's voice was extra cheery. She set down the roses and smiled at Alice. "Lucky lady." The brunette appeared to be around twenty, and she gave a little hum as she carefully touched the roses. "Someone must think you are very special."

Alice couldn't take her gaze off the roses.

"I'm Tiffany, by the way. I work in the gift shop."

She still couldn't look away from the flowers. "Who...who sent them?"

Tiffany laughed. "It's a surprise! Look at the card, and you'll see what I mean." Tiffany patted Alice's arm. "Feel better, you hear?" Tiffany's shoes didn't make a sound as she left, but she pulled the door shut with a hard *click*.

Alice reached out her hand, grasping the card that had been tucked inside the flowers. She pulled the card out of its small, white envelope.

Sorry I missed you. Next time, I won't.

Breathing became hard. Her heart nearly burst from her chest because the note ended with—

Your Secret Admirer.

Oh, hell no. Hell, *no*. Alice jumped from the bed. She wanted to throw those roses across the room. Instead, she ran for the door. She jerked it open, and the deputy who'd been assigned to be her shadow shoved away from the wall. "Ms. May?"

She ignored him, for the moment.

Alice bounded after Tiffany. Alice grabbed the other woman's shoulder and whipped her around. "*Who* sent the flowers?"

Tiffany gaped at her. "You don't like them?"

"*Who sent them?*"

The deputy was closing in. "Ms. May, calm down."

The hell she'd get calm.

"It was an-an online order," Tiffany stammered. "You fill out the request on the computer — we just get the flowers ready and print out the note. That's it. The note said 'Secret Admirer' and that's all I know!"

If the flowers had been ordered online, there had to be a way to trace the buyer. "Get the credit card number," Alice barked.

The deputy put his hand on Alice's shoulder. "You should let her go." His voice had hardened.

"She should get the credit card number!" Alice snapped back, but she let Tiffany go. Alice was trying her hardest not to freak out, but her control was holding by a thread.

The nearby elevator dinged, and the doors slid open. Zander marched out, but he came to a quick stop when he caught sight of Alice standing in the hallway, clad in her hospital gown.

"What's going on?" Zander demanded as he hurried closer to Alice.

Tiffany pointed at Alice. "She's acting crazy!" Her cheeks had turned blotchy. "I just—just delivered her some roses and she's—"

"They're from my Secret Admirer." Alice shoved the crumpled card at Zander. She'd fisted it in her left hand.

He took the card, unfolded it, and then swore. Dark, inventive words that she would have appreciated under different circumstances. Not then, though. Right then, she couldn't appreciate anything. She was too terrified.

Zander turned a lethal look onto the gift shop employee. "Who sent the flowers?"

Tiffany's eyes were the size of saucers. "I told her." She directed a pointed glance at Alice. "The order came in online. It was paid by credit card. I didn't *see* anyone!" She huffed out a hard breath. "Sorry you don't like the roses, lady, but it's just my job to deliver them."

No, she didn't like the roses. Alice wanted to rip them apart.

Zander pulled out his FBI badge. "I want that credit card number and anything else you've got on the guy who made this order. And I want that information *now*."

Tiffany wilted a bit. "What's happening?"

Oh, not too much…except that Alice was afraid a killer was stalking her. It very much looked as if the Secret Admirer had focused on a new victim…

And that victim is me.

***

The hospital room door opened again. Alice tensed and so did the deputy who'd been sent to keep watch over her.

Zander stalked into the room. His hard gaze swept over the deputy. "Give us a minute."

The deputy rushed out.

Alice crossed her arms over her chest. She'd changed back into her jeans and t-shirt. Shoved on her shoes. No way was she planning to stay longer in that hospital. She wanted out, right then.

Zander closed in on her, and the closer he got, the more she tensed.

"The sedan that almost hit you was stolen from a lady named Hannah Ivory. Turns out that Hannah's wallet was in the sedan when it was stolen. And the perp used her credit card to make the order for the flowers."

She tried to head around him and get out of the room.

Zander just side-stepped and blocked her path. "Alice, I need you to talk to me."

"And I need to get out of here."

Zander nodded. "I'm going to get you out. But...you aren't leaving on your own."

What?

His jaw locked. "The perp is targeting you. That's fucking obvious."

"Is it? Because I thought it was *obvious* that I was the killer. Isn't that what you think? What you and your buddy Randall think? That I'm a killer? That I was helping Hugh all along with his crimes?" She couldn't stop the torrent of words. "That I recently killed that poor woman, Julianna Stiles?"

"The perp left Julianna's necklace in the abandoned sedan."

Her lips parted, but Alice couldn't speak.

"He put it in the glove box, like he was leaving us some kind of present. He wanted us to know that he'd killed her. And he sent you the flowers because he wanted you to know that he was hunting you."

Her breath was heaving in and out. She rubbed her sweaty palms on her jean-clad legs. "My bedroom—"

His gaze was dark and grim. "If you hadn't come to my cabin last night, he would have found you in your room. And I think he would have killed you."

Her knees wanted to buckle. Shit, they *did* buckle, but Zander caught her. His strong hands closed around her shoulders.

"Baby?"

"No." She jerked away from him and the back of her legs hit the hospital bed. "Don't you dare 'baby' me right now. Don't act like we're close. Don't act like I matter to you."

I think he would have killed you.

"You *do* matter," Zander growled.

Such a lie. "I'm a case. I was a suspect, until, what—five minutes ago? An hour ago? Or for all I know, I'm *still* a suspect to you. Maybe you think I'm working some kind of major con job on you with a secret partner that I have hidden away some place." She couldn't let Zander keep standing that close to her. Her nerves were shot.

He exhaled slowly. "You were a suspect."

Well, he wasn't pulling punches, finally. And at least he'd said *were*, though she didn't completely buy the past tense idea. Alice wasn't going to put her trust in Zander any time soon.

"But right now, I think you're a victim." His gaze bored into her. "You're his next target, Alice. And I know you see that. Fuck, he *told* you that."

I won't miss you again.

"But I'm not letting that happen," Zander swore.

"Get out of my way, Zander." She *was* getting out of that room.

Zander shook his head. "You aren't leaving me."

"Zander—"

"Until we catch the bastard, you'll stay in federal custody. *My* custody."

"No." Alice shook her head. "Absolutely not. I will not—"

"I'm sorry, but you don't have an option here. Your life is on the line, and whether you like it or not, whether you like *me* or not, I'm not leaving you on your own. Not when this guy is fixated on you."

The flowers were gone. The roses had already been taken in as evidence. But her gaze still slid to the little table where they had rested before.

"You know how the Secret Admirer worked, Alice."

Her hands clenched at her sides. "This isn't Hugh. He's dead and buried, remember?"

"The authorities always considered the possibility that Hugh had an accomplice—"

"Me! The FBI thought it was me!"

He didn't deny her charge. "One year has passed. The bastard killed Julianna Stiles. And now, he's coming after you." Determination blazed in his eyes. "He's not getting to you, Alice. I'm not letting that happen. So if I have to handcuff you to my side, I will. But you aren't walking out of this hospital alone. Consider yourself in protective custody from this moment on. You'll be moved to a safe house, and you *will* remain safe. I'll be damned if I let you become his next victim."

***

Alice should have received his flowers by now. And the authorities — those clueless FBI agents and the foolish local deputies — would have found the sedan.

He'd needed to get their attention. The dumbasses had been going after Alice. As if she were the criminal.

Not Alice. Sweet Alice had been something altogether different.

He wouldn't have let her die in front of the sheriff's station. The intent had been to scare her. To make a show for the agents watching. So many FBI agents — they stuck out like a neon sign as they invaded the little office that passed for the sheriff's headquarters.

He'd wanted Alice to know he was there. Wanted everyone to know.

But he wouldn't have let her die that way. Not Alice. Alice wasn't like the others. She never had been. Alice was special, and he didn't think that she even realized the truth about everything that had happened...*all because of her.*

He would have swerved. Would have let her get across the street. But the fucking FBI agent had tried to play hero. He'd rushed after Alice. Swept her away.

Heroes got on his damn nerves.

Now, though, the agents would understand that he was the one pulling the strings. They'd know *he* had taken and killed Julianna. Alice shouldn't be treated like a criminal. Alice wasn't bad.

She was so very good. Perfect, in fact.

For a whole year, he'd watched her. Alice had stayed true to Hugh's memory. She hadn't dated anyone. Hadn't screwed the horny bastards who'd chased after her. No tell-all books had been written by sweet Alice, though he knew she'd gotten plenty of offers. She'd kept her silence. Hadn't gone out of her way to make Hugh look like a monster.

The Press had been busy doing their own job of that.

No, Alice had held her silence. She'd kept her secrets.

Perfect Alice.

That was why he'd gone to her the night before. But...

Where were you, Alice? He still didn't know that answer, but he'd be asking Alice, soon enough. When he hadn't found Alice in her cabin, his rage had taken over.

He was in control now, though.

And he'd keep his control, until he was with Alice again. He couldn't wait to see her. To touch her. To own her.

His Alice.

A whole year had passed. Time for Alice to end her grief. Mourning was over.

Alice could love again. She could — she *would* — love him.

After all, he'd been waiting so patiently for her.

CHAPTER SEVEN

"Your cabin?" Alice stared at Zander with her wide, deep blue eyes. Her hands were fisted as they rested on her hips. "If you think I'm staying here with you tonight, you're crazy."

"Why?" This low question came from Randall, not Zander. "You stayed with him last night."

Alice's gaze cut to the other FBI agent. "Let's be clear." She gave an ice-cold smile to him. "I don't like you. This morning, you were ready to lock me in a jail cell and call me guilty."

Randall shoved his hands into the pockets of his pants as he rocked forward. "Yeah about that..." He gave a faint shrug. "I'm still not convinced that you're one hundred percent innocent."

No, the guy wasn't. Randall had been arguing the possibility of her involvement with the perp for most of the evening. And Zander had argued back just as fiercely as he defended her.

"If you *are* innocent, though," Randall continued with a slow nod, "then this is the perfect chance for you to do your civic duty."

"My duty?" Alice's delicate brows rose.

Randall smiled like a shark. "Help us catch the bastard."

Alice sucked in a sharp breath. Immediately, her gaze flew back to Zander. He almost winced at the fury he saw in her stare. "Is that the plan? Use me to catch him?"

He should tread carefully. He didn't want to lie to her again. He wanted her trust back, and Zander knew that was going to be one hell of a battle. He'd shattered her faith in him. And he hadn't even realized that would damn well hurt him, not until he'd walked into that closet of an interrogation room at the sheriff's station...and Alice had stared at him as if he were a total stranger to her.

Because that's exactly what I am.

"Is that the plan?" Alice pushed as she strode closer. Her scent—light jasmine—seemed to envelope him. "I thought you said I was in protective custody. You never mentioned I was bait."

His back teeth had locked. With an effort, Zander unclenched them. "I want to keep you safe. This cabin is secure. No one is going to get close without my team knowing."

"Am I bait?" Her voice was low, husky.

And he was an asshole. "We think he will come after you. It's obvious, based on what he's already done—"

Her mocking laughter cut him off. It was so different from the few, precious laughs she'd given him before. Now her laughter was flat and hard. Bitter. "Then I guess I'm doing my civic duty, huh? Whether I like it or not." Her hands fell to her sides. "Here's the thing, though. For the record…" Her chin notched up. "I would have volunteered to do this. You didn't have to lie to me about wanting me to be safe. Didn't have to keep pretending. I want to stop this guy. I would have stopped Hugh, if I'd known the truth, and there is no way I can just sit back and let this monster kill someone else. If I can do anything to stop him, I will." Her shoulders rolled back. "So maybe stop lying to me, and just bring me in on the plan, okay?"

She'd surprised Randall. Zander could see it, though the other agent worked hard to school his expression.

"All right." Zander paced away from her. His gaze cut to the window. Darkness was already falling. Darkness came early in the mountains. "We think he'll try going to your place first. We'll have a female agent inside, someone who looks like you. Cara McCoy is well-trained, and she'll be ready for any attack that comes her way."

"We'll be watching the place," Randall added quickly. "Our agents have eyes on it. We'll know if he's getting close. The minute he steps inside, he'll be ours."

Zander glanced back at Alice. A furrow had appeared between her brows. "Doesn't sound like you're using me as bait," she murmured. "Sounds like this Cara — she's the bait."

"There was a...pattern to the Secret Admirer's attacks before," Zander began carefully. "He sent his victims flowers — "

"Just like the roses I got in the hospital, yes, I know." She began to pace. "He saw someone who caught his eye. He tried romance first. Sent his target flowers. He locked on to her social media profile. Learned everything he could about the woman." She stilled. "I'm not online. Not anymore."

So the perp would advance to the next step. "He sent texts to his victims. He called them." Always from a burner phone. Something they'd learned *after* the victims had died, and they'd gone through the phone records. "He preferred to call at night, when they were at home, sometimes when they were even in bed."

She flinched.

And he remembered...she'd been questioned about those calls. Because according to her own accounts, Hugh had been with her at the same time that some of the calls had been placed.

Either the guy had snuck out of the bedroom, getting a few moments of secrecy...or there had been a partner. Someone *else* who'd made the phone calls when Hugh had been with Alice.

"He'll call you," Zander murmured. He wanted to get closer to her, but every time he did, she tensed. So he stayed near the window. "We want you to talk to him. Keep him on the line. Draw him in."

Randall nodded. "If you keep him talking, then maybe we'll get lucky and be able to trace him through the call."

Yeah, that was option one. Option two, though...the perp would make the call, then he'd go to Alice's cabin. Inside, he'd find Cara waiting.

"And in the meantime, you stay with me," Zander said. *Because I want you close. Protected.* "You stay here where I can keep an eye on you. You stay safe. You stay with me, until we end this thing."

She crossed her arms over her chest. Resumed pacing. "This Cara — she'll be safe? You're sure of this?"

It was Randall who answered, "She's a trained FBI agent. She can handle herself."

Alice tucked a lock of hair behind her ear. "He's going to be angry when he goes in and doesn't find me."

Yes, he would be. They were counting on his rage.

"Angry people make mistakes. This bastard is going down." Randall's face hardened with determination. "Because I'll be damned if I have to look into the eyes of another grieving family and tell them that this bastard took away someone they loved."

***

"You're safe."

Alice jumped when she heard the low rumble of Zander's voice behind her. She'd been staring into the fireplace, lost in those flickering flames, and she hadn't even heard his approach.

He cursed, then said, "Didn't mean to scare you."

Then maybe don't walk up behind me when a killer is on the loose.

They were alone in his cabin. Randall had left over an hour before. Clothes had been brought to her. Toiletries. All the comforts of home. Enough supplies to last for days. Because no one seemed to know how long this little visit with Zander would last.

Zander had started the fire. It wasn't cold outside, so she didn't even know why he'd lit it. Maybe the guy had thought the flames were soothing? If that was the case, he was dead wrong.

"Alice?"

She made herself turn to face him. "I'm not scared of you."

His eyes narrowed. "No, you're just pissed as all hell, aren't you?"

Pissed? "Not quite a strong enough word." Her chin lifted. "I don't exactly like it when men use sex to try and manipulate me." She pushed past him.

But he caught her wrist and spun her back around to face him. "That's not what happened."

"No? From where I stand, it sure as hell seems to be." And it wasn't just rage that she felt. Pain. The pain was the worst. Because she'd believed he was someone she could trust. But she'd put all the puzzle pieces together and realized how truly foolish she'd been. "How many lies have you told me?"

"Alice—"

"You know, I was thinking about it...so incredibly convenient, wasn't it, that I needed all of those repairs at my place?"

A muscle jerked in his jaw. "Wasn't convenient."

No, she hadn't thought it was. "You did that," Alice accused. "You broke those things, just so I'd call you. So I'd need you." Damn him. *Damn him.* "You weren't helping me. You were trying to trick me all along. And I was so stupidly grateful for everything you did. So glad that I'd found someone who seemed *nice.*"

His stare was cold. Hard. "I had a job to do."

She backed up a step. That jab *hurt*. "Then I guess you did it." He'd fucked her for the FBI. Talk about taking one for the team. She glanced down at his hand. "Let me go."

He pulled her closer. "I didn't want to cross the line with you."

Was she supposed to believe that?

"I tried to stay away from you. I was sleeping on the couch, remember? No, not sleeping. Because I couldn't sleep. If you want the damn truth, I haven't had a good night's sleep since I met you."

Jerk. "So sorry for the inconvenience."

His hold tightened on her wrist. "You are in my head. When I close my eyes, I see you. Your smile. The way your face gets all serious and you get a little furrow between your brows when you're thinking hard about something."

"Let go of my hand."

"I wanted you from the first moment because you are fucking gorgeous. But you got beneath my skin..." He tugged her even closer. "You did that because you are strong, and you're smart and you're—"

"A killer? Isn't that what you thought when we first met?" And it *hurt*. "How can someone like you want a killer?"

"I was supposed to prove your guilt," he gritted out.

The words were like nails in her coffin. She snatched her hand from his grip. Took two quick steps back.

"I was supposed to prove your guilt...or find a way to show the world you were innocent. Know which option I wanted? Know why I was awake at night? Every single night? Because I needed you to be innocent. I wanted to prove that—not your guilt."

Did he think she'd believe his lies again? *Not today.*

"I knew I should have kept my hands off you. I fucking tried." His hands were fisted right then. "But last night, when you came to my door...you were wet from the rain, and you were the most beautiful thing I'd ever seen."

She didn't want to hear more. "Stop."

"I intended to sleep on the couch. Having sex with you—that was a line I wasn't going to cross. Then you screamed."

Alice turned away from him. She'd screamed, and he'd come running into the bedroom. She'd been the one to say she wanted him. She'd been the one to push.

"You were scared, and I hated your fear. I wanted to take it all away. I wanted you to *never* fear again." His voice rasped behind her. "And I wanted you. More than I've ever wanted anyone or anything in my life."

She wasn't going to believe him. Zander had already proved he was a world class liar.

Just like Hugh.

No, no, dammit, he's not like Hugh.

"I wasn't going to leave you. Nothing could have made me leave you."

She put one foot in front of the other as she headed for the stairs.

"Alice?"

Her shoulders stiffened.

"I'm sorry, Alice."

Her eyes closed.

"Hurting you was never part of my plan."

Her eyes opened. She climbed the first step. The second. The third. Behind her, she heard him stalk toward the stairs, and she stopped, making herself turn and look at him. "You didn't want to hurt me." Her chest burned. "What did you think would happen when I found out the truth?"

She saw a flash of torment on his face.

"Alice—"

"But it was just part of the job, right? Everything was part of the job." She gave a careless shrug even though careless was the last thing she felt. "Except for the fucking part. That was a bonus."

He bounded up the stairs. Crowded too close to her. She thought he'd wrap his hands around her arms again. That he'd try to justify—

"I am an asshole. You think I don't know that?" His eyes blazed. "I'm sorry I hurt you. You can bet your life that it won't happen again. No more lies. You're only going to get the truth from me, from here on out. And you might not always like what I have to say, but I won't ever deceive you again."

"That's great." Her voice was deliberately mocking even as her heart raced.

"*You* matter. What we did last night? It matters, too. I'm going to prove myself to you."

"Why?" They were done. Over. They had barely started their relationship — or whatever the hell it had been — and it had already ended. "I'm just a case. When the killer is caught, you won't ever see me again." She'd never see him.

Case closed.

But Zander shook his head. A faint smile teased his lips. "Baby, you are so much more than just a case." His hand lifted, as if he'd touch her cheek, but his fingers stilled in the air. A moment later, his hand fisted once again as his arm fell back to his side. "I'm going to prove myself, because I want a real chance with you."

Why was he jerking her around? "I'm going to bed. Taking *your* bed. You sleep on the couch." She hurried up several stairs.

"I didn't fake my reaction to you. I didn't fake the way you make me feel."

She didn't stop.

"I will never hurt you again. I swear it."

She was at the top of the stairs. Hurriedly, Alice turned to the right. She rushed into his bedroom. Slammed the door shut.

I will never hurt you again.

If only she could believe those words. Unfortunately, it seemed that she had a very dangerous tendency to pick lovers…who lied.

***

He stayed on the stairs too long. His gaze was directed up at the closed bedroom door.

He was such a damn bastard.

I'm sorry, Alice.

Had there been tears in her eyes? He thought he'd seen them. He didn't want Alice crying. He sure as hell didn't want to be the man who *made* her cry.

Alice should smile. Alice should laugh. She should be happy.

Give me a chance, baby. I can prove to you that I can be more than just another SOB who has hurt you. Because Alice mattered. She'd gotten beneath his skin. And the night before…*I've never wanted anyone that badly.*

Hell, Alice wasn't just beneath his skin. He thought she might be in his heart.

Only he hadn't realized the truth, hadn't even realized that he was falling for Alice, not until she'd looked at him with betrayal in her eyes.

Then he'd understood that he'd destroyed something very special. Something he hadn't even known was there, not until it was too late.

I can fix this. Just give me the chance.

His phone rang, the shrill cry making him swear as he hurried to grab the device from the table near the couch. He recognized the ring tone as Randall's, and he shoved the phone to his ear. "Everyone in position?"

"We are set." Randall's voice was low. "Cara is in the cabin. We've got eyes on the place, and if the bastard makes a move tonight, we've got him."

But he might not make a move that night. He might not make a move for days, or weeks. And if that happened…

I'm not going to leave Alice unprotected.

"Everything okay on your end?" Randall prompted.

Hell, no, things were not okay. "I'll take care of Alice." Even if she hated him.

He ended the call. Went to the couch. Put his gun and his phone on the coffee table. Then Zander made his ass comfortable. Not like he'd be going anywhere, not anytime soon.

***

The FBI agents were such fools. Did they think he didn't realize they were there? That he didn't know a trap when he saw one?

He spotted the agents easily as they hid in the woods. One dumbass was even smoking. Like the scent of the smoke wouldn't travel on the wind. He saw them, counted them. Knew what they were doing.

They wanted to pull him in. They thought that when he stepped foot in Alice's cabin, they'd have him.

He wasn't going inside. Not yet.

He retreated, slipping away from the cabin. Making sure no one saw him. Making sure that he was out of sight. It was time to talk with Alice.

But he wasn't going in her home.

He was going to get his sweet Alice...to come to him.

CHAPTER EIGHT

The phone rang, jarring Alice from the light sleep she'd finally managed to get. She was in Zander's bed, fully dressed and on top of the covers, and when her phone rang, she jerked upright.

It rang again and vibrated across the bedside table. She flipped on the light and reached for her phone even as the bedroom door flew open.

Zander had gotten there fast. Very fast.

As if he'd just been standing right outside of the bedroom door.

She looked at the screen. "*Unknown caller.*" Her stomach immediately clenched. *Oh, God. This is it.*

Zander hurried toward the bed. "Put it on speaker when you answer the call."

She nodded and swallowed the lump in her throat. Her finger slid across the phone's screen as she answered, and she quickly tapped the option to put the caller on speaker. "H-hello?" She hated the stutter of her voice, but Alice was afraid.

Silence. No...wait, had that been the rush of wind?

Zander motioned with his hand for her to speak again.

"Hello?" Her voice was stronger now. "Who is this?"

"Did you get my flowers?"

She sucked in a sharp breath. The voice was robotic, and she knew the caller was using some sort of distorter.

"Alice, I've missed you."

"Who is this?" Alice demanded again.

He laughed. Because of the robotic sound, the laughter was like nails sliding down a chalkboard. "You know."

"No, I have no clue." She found herself staring at Zander. Somehow, looking into his eyes helped to calm her fear. "And I don't have your flowers. The FBI has them."

More laughter. "Of course, I wanted them to know I was here."

Here...in the same town with her. Hunting her.

"And you know who I am, Alice." The volume of the voice decreased. A rough, metallic whisper told her, "I'm your Secret Admirer."

Goosebumps covered her arms. She was supposed to keep the guy talking. Zander had sent out a text as soon as she picked up the phone, and Alice knew the FBI agents were trying to track the call. She had to keep the guy talking. "Hugh Collins was the Secret Admirer. He's dead. He's—"

"Was he?" More of that laughter. "I'm *your* Secret Admirer. I think you're perfect, Alice. Absolutely perfect."

Her breath sawed in and out, and she knew he'd hear the desperate pants. "Where are you?"

"Look out your bedroom window, and you'll see."

What?

She saw Zander fire out a quick text.

"Come on, Alice. Do it. Look out your window and tell me what you see."

She didn't know what to do. Obviously, she couldn't look out her window. She wasn't in her bedroom. Agent Cara McCoy was in her bedroom. "I'm not playing your game." There. That sounded good. "I'm hanging up the phone, and I'm calling the authorities. You stay away from me, do you understand? Keep your sick, twisted—"

"She'll die."

Alice's heart seemed to stop.

"She's not you. None of them were *you,* and I'm tired of the weak substitutes. So I'll trade. You for her."

"Who?" Her voice was too high. Too shocked. Too scared.

Zander reached for her left hand. His fingers curled around hers.

"Dark hair. Blue eyes. She even walked like you. When I saw her today...well, after she delivered the flowers to you in the hospital, I thought...she'd be perfect."

No, *no.*

"I haven't hurt her, not yet. But I will."

"*Don't.*"

"Then trade. You for her. It's easy."

Zander shook his head.

"Where? When?" Alice blurted.

"Right here. Right now. Come out of the cabin. Walk to me. When I have you, I'll tell the cops where Tiffany is. Come to me."

The line went dead.

Oh, hell, *no.*

Alice leapt out of the bed. She ran for the door.

But Zander grabbed her. He locked his arms around her waist and yanked her back against his body. "No! Jesus, no, baby, you *aren't* going out there!"

She fought against his hold, but he just held her tighter. "He has the woman from the hospital! Tiffany!" Alice could see the other woman so clearly in her mind. "I can't let her die!"

"She won't." Zander's breath blew against her ear. "Your call was being monitored. You know that. And I was texting Randall the whole time. Cara will go out of the cabin, just like the bastard ordered. But Cara will be armed. She'll run out just as if she's you."

Her breath heaved in and out.

"It's going to be okay," Zander said. "We've got this."

***

Special Agent Cara McCoy adjusted her ear piece, and then she made sure that her weapon was concealed beneath her coat. She pulled in a deep breath, squared her shoulders, and got her ass in character.

When she opened the front door and ran outside, fear was clear on her face. She let the terror show. She rushed toward the woods and spun in a circle. "I'm here!" Cara yelled. *"Where are you?"* Frantically, she turned, trying to move quickly so that anyone watching wouldn't get a too-close look at her face. But she wasn't too worried. It was dark. The watcher wouldn't be able to see her very clearly.

She just needed to find him...

***

Alice's phone rang again.

Zander saw her stiffen, and her gaze immediately shot to the phone that she'd tossed on the bed moments before. Zander had already released her. As soon as she'd stopped fighting, he'd let her go, and now he watched as she hurried to scoop up her phone.

"Unknown caller," Alice whispered. "It's him again."

"Don't," Zander snapped out the quick command. "Cara should be outside by now. If you answer it and he's watching, he'll know we're tricking him."

Her stare was on the phone. "If I don't answer it, what happens to the woman he took?"

Zander shook his head. "If he is watching Cara, if he's out there like he said…" And he hoped the sonofabitch was. If the guy was in the woods…*the agents will find you.* "Then he'll see that she doesn't answer. He'll see every move Cara makes. He'll just think you ran out of the cabin so fast you forgot your phone. But if you answer…"

The phone rang again.

"If you answer the phone right now, you blow the whole show."

***

Cara couldn't see anyone in the woods. She knew that other agents were stationed out there. Watching. Waiting. They were all searching for the perp. She stepped closer to the edge of the woods. Should she go into the trees? Walk through the darkness?

If he was out there, he'd see what she did. Whatever move she made, perhaps he would follow.

Cara hesitated. She didn't want to walk into his trap.

She wanted him to walk into hers.

She turned around. Headed back for the cabin. She made sure her steps were slow, hesitant. Right before she reached the porch, Cara stopped. She turned back toward the darkness. "If you're here, show yourself!"

Something hit her chest. Hard and fast, and Cara stumbled. She blinked, then looked down. Her hand rose...and touched the blood. Blood that poured from the wound in her chest.

Then she fell.

***

The phone rang, and Alice jumped.

Only...it wasn't her phone ringing. It was Zander's. He yanked up the phone, knowing by the ring tone that Randall was calling. "Tell me you got the bastard."

"No." Randall's voice cracked. "The sonofabitch. He *shot* Cara."

"What?"

Alice edged closer. Zander hadn't put the call on speaker, but Randall's voice was loud, and Zander knew Alice would be able to hear most of the words his partner was saying.

"She was near the porch. She was calling out to him. A bullet slammed into her chest." Randall's ragged breathing drifted over the line. "She's...shit...it hit her heart. We're working on her, trying to get an ambulance out here but...*shit*," he snarled again. "This isn't his MO! He doesn't shoot his victims. If we'd fucking thought he'd shoot, Cara would've worn her vest!"

No, the Secret Admirer never shot his victims. But he also didn't try to run them down with cars, either. *Yet Alice had almost been hit by the sedan.* This time, the killer was different. *Because we aren't dealing with Hugh Collins. This is a different sonofabitch.* So this killer was playing by a different set of rules.

"Keep Alice close," Randall urged.

Like Zander had to be told that. There was no way Alice would get away from him. He ended the call.

Alice's eyes were huge. "H-he *shot* her?"

Zander nodded.

"Is she...is she okay?"

No, he didn't think that Cara was okay. Not based on what Randall had told him. Dammit.

Alice's phone rang. She grabbed it from the bed. "It's him."

Zander's fingers closed around hers. "Don't answer it. Fucking don't."

"We have to find the missing woman!" Alice snapped.

If she was missing. If the perp's words hadn't been a lie. A trap. He'd sent a text earlier ordering deputies over to the home of the suspected victim, Tiffany Shaw. They were searching for her.

Zander didn't want Alice talking to the bastard right then. "Let me talk to him."

"But—"

"Maybe he thinks you're dead, Alice. Maybe he thinks he just shot you."

She let go of the phone.

Zander's fingers slid over the screen, and he put the phone on speaker. "Who the fuck is this?"

Grating robotic laughter was his answer. Then... "That wasn't Alice."

"Listen, you—"

"She didn't walk like Alice. And her voice, when she called out—*wasn't* Alice's voice."

The bastard had been close enough to hear Cara. He'd been right there, and the agents in the woods had missed him. "You're done. Do you hear me? Agents are closing in. They're coming after you—"

"No, they're too busy trying to save the woman. I'm a good shot. Very good. So they won't save her. But at least they're trying. Good for them."

All of the color bled from Alice's face.

The robotic voice demanded, "Where is my Alice?"

Zander stared straight at her. "You'll never touch Alice."

"Then I guess Tiffany Shaw will be dying. I'll use my knife on her. She's very much a disappointment. Started begging and crying the instant I took off the hood I'd shoved over her head. I didn't want her. I never wanted her. It's always been Alice."

Always been Alice. Fucking hell.

"Where. Is. Alice?"

Zander knew that he had to keep the guy talking. His team could trace the call. They could *find* him. "You're just some wannabe," Zander taunted. "The real Secret Admirer doesn't shoot his victims. But then, the real guy is dead, isn't he? So what are you? Just some copycat? Some dumb prick who can't even get the MO right?"

"If I don't talk to Alice, I'll send Tiffany to you in pieces."

"*I'm here!*" Alice cried out.

Fuck. Zander's back teeth ground together. Silence.

The robotic voice said, "I'm very angry with you, Alice."

Her eyes were huge. "Really? Because I don't care. Let Tiffany go. Don't hurt—"

"I waited for you, my perfect Alice. But when I came to you, you weren't there."

Zander's phone vibrated. He glanced down at the text. Not from Randall, but from another team member. *Triangulating signal.*

Hell, yes.

"Where were you, Alice?" the distorted voice demanded.

Zander's phone vibrated again. *Within five hundred feet of your location.*

The bastard was still in the woods. Waiting and watching. Agents were crawling through the trees. They'd find him. He'd *better* not get away.

"Where were you?" Even distorted, the rage was clear. "And who the fuck were you with?"

"Me, asshole," Zander snarled back to him. "She was with me."

The call went dead. Alice dropped her phone onto the bed.

Fury blasted through Zander. "He's still in the woods. The team traced his call. He's within five hundred feet of this cabin." And that was why he'd told the guy that she was with him. If the guy had been watching Alice—and watching had been such a part of the original Secret

Admirer's pattern — then he'd know where Zander's cabin was. He'd come there.

Come inside, bastard. Come closer.

Zander bounded down the stairs. Alice rushed after him. "Why did you do that?"

He grabbed his gun. Turned toward her. "Because I don't want him fixated on you. I don't want him shooting other agents. I don't want him hurting that woman from the hospital." His jaw locked. "If the bastard wants to hurt someone, he needs to focus on me. Because I will sure as fuck hurt him back."

***

The killer didn't call again. Four hours passed, and there was nothing. The woods were searched. The agents had even brought in the K9 unit. At first, the dogs had a scent, but they lost it near the river.

The bastard had disappeared into thin air.

Cara had been pronounced dead at the scene. The bullet had torn straight through her heart. The agents had figured out the angle of entry, the trajectory, located the exact spot the guy must have been standing in when he took the shot —

But they hadn't found him.

The sonofabitch was still out there. And that meant Alice wasn't safe.

Zander sat on the couch, his eyes on the remnants of the fire. Faint embers glowed in the dark.

The stairs creaked behind him.

He rolled back his shoulders. "You should be sleeping."

"She died in my place."

He turned his head. Alice had her arms wrapped around her stomach. Her head tipped forward, and her long hair trailed over her shoulders.

"I keep thinking about that. About her. He was in the woods because he wanted me. When he didn't get me..."

It's always been Alice.

Zander rose. He stalked toward the kitchen and pulled out his whiskey. He poured a glass and headed back for the den. Alice had moved closer to the fireplace. She gazed down at the embers. "I think you could use a drink," he muttered.

She glanced up at him. "I think they all died in my place."

"This *isn't* on you. It's on him. Okay? He's the freak who took those women — "

"Did he really take Tiffany? Did Randall find out? Did he talk to her family?"

"Tiffany lives alone. Deputies went to her apartment, but she wasn't there. There was no sign of a forced entry at her place, and her neighbors said she hadn't been home."

Alice hadn't taken the whiskey.

Zander sighed. "Cameras and footage are being checked from the hospital. It's possible that he took her from there." *He'd been at the hospital, and the guy might have even seen Alice when she'd been there.*

She grabbed the whiskey. Took a gulp. Shuddered. "That tastes horrible."

Zander grunted. "It's an acquired taste."

"To be clear, I will never acquire it."

His lips twisted into a half-smile.

She didn't smile back. "I'm going to make the trade." She pushed the glass of whiskey back at him.

And the faint curve of his lips vanished. "What?"

"I'm making the trade. When he calls again, *if* he calls again, I'm telling him that I'll do it. I'll go wherever he wants, I'll do what he wants, but I'm not going to let Tiffany die in my place."

"I don't happen to like this plan." Under-fucking-statement.

"Too bad. It's not about what you want or what you like."

Had she forgotten the whole protective custody part? That he was the agent and she was the civilian? She wasn't supposed to give him orders. Not exactly the way the system worked.

"That agent wasn't supposed to die tonight." Her lashes swept toward her cheeks. "Another death, another mark on my soul. Do you have any idea what it is like? The guilt that eats at me? She was in my cabin. Wearing my clothes. Pretending to be *me*."

But Cara had died because she *wasn't* Alice. Because the perp knew Alice so well that he could tell by the agent's walk that she wasn't the woman he wanted.

Alice brushed past him and headed for the stairs.

He put down the glass before he crushed it. Rage and fear twisted inside of him. "I've been watching you, Alice."

Her shoulders stiffened.

"At first, watching you was my job. I was supposed to learn your routine. To learn who you were. What you liked."

She turned to face him.

"I learned what you liked, and I gave you what you wanted. That was the way I got close to you. I was there, even when you didn't know it." He inclined his head. "But I wasn't the only one. He was watching you, too. The perp we're after. The one who has a fucking obsession with you." An obsession so deep that the guy killed other women who weren't the real Alice May. *Because he doesn't want a substitute. He wants you.* "I think he's been watching you for a very long time. He *knows* you, Alice."

Zander could hear the catch in her breathing.

"And I think that means you know him, too." Because the way the guy acted with Alice—it was so focused. So fixated. "He would need to be close to you. He's someone that you've talked with before. That's why he disguised his voice. He didn't want you to recognize it."

She shook her head. "I—you're wrong. I've barely spoken to anyone while I've been up here. You—you're the only one I've gotten close to—"

"He's not someone new, Alice. Not someone you met up here. He's someone from your life in Savannah. Back when you were with Hugh. He's someone who has been in your life for a very long time." Zander closed in on her. Alice's head tipped back as she stared up at him, and he had to clench his hands into fists so that he wouldn't reach out and touch her.

If he touched her, he'd want to take her.

No, fuck it, he *already* wanted to take her. He had his own obsession when it came to Alice May. Only he wasn't a twisted sonofabitch who got off on murder.

"You know who he is," Zander stated flatly. "He's been in your life all along. He's hooked on you, and he's not going to give you up. No matter what he has to do," *or who he has to kill,* "he won't let you go."

***

Alice had been perfect. His beautiful Alice.

She'd mourned Hugh. Even with the stories circulating in the news, even with the evidence, she'd cried at his funeral.

She hadn't gone to the news and spread stories about how twisted Hugh had been. Hadn't taken the book offers that he knew she'd been given.

He knew so much about Alice.

Because he watched her so much.

One whole year had passed since Hugh had been put into the ground, and during that time, Alice had stayed faithful. No other men. No lovers at all.

Until the one-year anniversary.

Until he'd gone to her cabin, ready to see her. Ready to touch her. *Finally,* ready to take what should have always been his.

He'd watched her. She'd had that fool in her cabin earlier that night, but she'd sent him away. The agent who lied to her. The agent who'd pretended to be someone else.

She'd sent him away.

"Me, asshole. She was with me." Special Agent Zander Todd's voice rang in his head again.

Alice had gone to Zander Todd. She'd rushed to him in the storm. She'd spent the night with him.

Alice…why?

She'd been so perfect. He'd thought she was different. That she could be trusted. That she was going to be *his*.

He glanced down at the knife in his hand. The blade gleamed, sharp and long.

Alice, you should have been perfect.

The old floor groaned beneath his feet as he made his way to the bedroom. His right hand clenched tightly around the knife, and his left rose to close around the handle of the bedroom door. The door slid open with a squeak, and there she was.

Dark hair.

Blue eyes.

Porcelain skin.

Younger than Alice. Smaller.

But he could imagine…as he'd done with the others…he could *see* his Alice in her… "Why the fuck did you go to him?"

Her eyes widened.

"You were meant for me." He rushed toward the bed.

CHAPTER NINE

"He's obsessed." Zander stared down at her with his dark, stormy eyes. "Don't you see that? Come on, Alice. They all look like you. The Secret Admirer killings *started* when Hugh met you. Those women died—"

"Because they looked like me." Her breath came too fast. Her heart raced in her chest. "Yes, I know that." And it tore her apart. "That's why I'm going to make the trade. I'm sick of people dying in my place. It has to stop." Her voice rose with each word. Her control—the careful control that she'd kept so tightly for the last year—was shredding around her. "No one else is going to die for me. When he calls, I'll get a location. I'll go to him. And maybe it will all just end." The way it should have ended when Hugh's casket was lowered into the ground. But it hadn't. The nightmare was still going on.

Either because the Feds were right—and Hugh's partner was still hunting. *He had a partner all along…*

Or because some sicko had started a copycat routine.

Either way…*It has to end.*

She spun on her heel and headed for the stairs once more. But she'd only taken two steps before Zander caught her. He turned her toward him, pulled her close, and she stumbled, her body pressing against his.

"You think I'm going to let you risk your life?" he growled.

"You think I'm giving you a choice?" Alice threw right back. "I tried it your way. We sent that agent to my cabin, and she *died*." No more. No one else could die in her place.

"So you're ready to die instead?" Anger was there, biting in each word that Zander spoke. "Not on my fucking watch." The storm in his eyes raged harder. "You do not die. You *do not*."

She opened her mouth to reply, but his lips were on hers. The kiss was wild and angry and rough. And she should have shoved against his chest. Should have told him to back the hell away.

But instead, it was as if something ignited inside of her. Her emotions were an utter wreck. She was still furious at Zander for his lies, for his betrayal. She was scared because of the bastard hunting her. She was sad and guilty because of the agent who'd been shot…

Alice was…God, she *hurt*.

And when he kissed her, when she felt the surge of passion and desire rise within her, Alice just—

She let go of all the fear and the pain, and she grabbed tightly to Zander. Her hands curled around his shoulders. Her nails dug into the soft, cotton fabric of his t-shirt. Her mouth opened wider, and their tongues met. Need exploded. She didn't think about what had been or what *would* be. The moment mattered.

There was nothing past *this* moment.

They tore off each other's clothes. He stripped away her bra, tossed it aside. Then he was lifting her up, holding her with a surprising strength that was incredibly sexy as his mouth closed around her breast. He took two steps, and she felt the wood of the wall against her back. He was licking her nipple. Sucking. Stroking. And her moans came fast and hard.

Her legs wrapped around him. She just wore a scrap of cotton underwear. His shirt was gone, but he was still clad in his jeans. She wanted to be skin to skin. Wanted him in her, right then. No time for thinking. No time for hesitating. No time for anything but pleasure.

He kissed his way to her other breast. Her hips surged against him, rocking in a desperate, needy rhythm. Desire fueled her blood. She wanted him. Wanted to see if the pleasure would still be as good this time. Maybe it had been a fluke before. Maybe—

He lifted his head. Lowered her so that her toes touched the floor. "Do you want this?" His voice was gravel-rough. His eyes seemed to devour her. "Do you want me?"

"Yes." She couldn't imagine wanting anyone more.

His eye blazed. "I won't mess up again with you. You can count on me."

"Zander..."

"I'll prove myself to you." His right hand slid between their bodies. His knuckles stroked the crotch of her panties. The panties were wet, she knew it. She was wet. Wet, ready, and so eager. Alice wanted him. Needed him.

"Zander, *now*."

He yanked at the panties. When they tore from her, she thought it was sexy as hell. Wild. That was how he made her feel. She fumbled, reaching between them, and she jerked open the button of his jeans. The zipper slid down with a low hiss. Then his cock was shoving into her hands. No underwear for her special agent. His heavy length surged toward her, and she stroked him, pumping his cock, and he let out a low hiss.

"*Baby,* I'm going fucking insane."

That made two of them.

He lifted her again, positioning himself at the entrance to her body. The head of his erection pushed against her. Her breath panted out —

"*Fuck. Condom.*"

Oh, jeez, she'd almost forgotten. She'd stopped taking birth control over the last year, and she needed —

"Hold on tight, baby."

She locked her arms around his shoulders. And he carried her up the stairs. With her legs still wrapped around his hips, with his cock right there, sliding over her sensitive core, making her moan and ache, he rushed up the stairs.

Then they were in his bedroom. He lowered her onto the bed. "Don't move."

Like she had to be told that. Alice was going *crazy.* Her legs parted for him. "Hurry!"

He grabbed a condom from the nightstand drawer. Put the thing on in a flash, then surged toward her. "Can't go slow," Zander gasped. "*Need...you.*"

He thrust into her. She almost came. Right there. That fast. He filled her completely, and her nails raked down his back. So good. Dammit, even better than before. Even better.

He withdrew. Thrust deep. Their rhythm was fast and hard, and they rolled over the bed. She was on top now, and her knees pushed into the mattress. Her hands flattened on his chest as she rose up and down, taking him in deep, and his fingers pressed to her clit. Caressing her. Driving her toward her orgasm—

The climax shook her whole body. She didn't even have the breath to cry out when it hit her. Alice stiffened, then shuddered, as pleasure pounded through her on wave after wave of release.

"You are the most beautiful thing I've ever seen." His words were guttural. Then he was surging up. She tumbled back, and he drove even deeper into her. He lifted her legs, putting them over his shoulders, and he came, plunging hard into her. Calling out her name. Holding her so tight.

In the aftermath, Alice struggled to catch her breath. He was on top of her, the bedding was bunched beneath her, and he was still *in* her. Her control was gone. All of the careful barriers that she'd put up to protect herself from pain and betrayal were gone.

It was just her.

Just him.

Zander lifted his head. He stared at her a moment, not saying a word.

She wasn't looking for any kind of forever. Didn't expect some magical words from him that said—

"I will never lie to you again, Alice May."

Her heart had just slowed down, but at his words, her heart rate doubled.

"I will not betray you. I will be someone you can trust."

She had to blink because suddenly, he'd gone a little blurry on her.

"I am sorry I hurt you. I would sooner cut off my own arm than hurt you."

Her lips pressed together.

"I will never hurt you again." He stared at her. "And one day...one day, you will believe in me." His lips twisted. "And if I'm really fucking lucky, maybe you'll even love me."

What? "Zander—"

"Not today. I know." His smile stretched just a little, and her chest felt funny. Probably because her heart was thundering so fast. "But we're going to have all the time in the world. You'll see that. I'm going to protect you. I'm going to stop this bastard. And then, Alice May, will you do me the honor of dating me?"

She laughed. The sound felt alien to her. But in that moment, the laughter just escaped. She felt happiness trickle through her. The sweet, poignancy of...*what if.*

It would be so nice to let go. To try falling for someone new again. To think of a future.

But her laughter died away because Alice knew she might not have a future. The picket fence and Friday night football routine might not be in the cards for her.

She was going to end the nightmare. She was going to meet her Secret Admirer. Only she might not be walking away from that meeting.

But she didn't tell Zander those things. Alice swallowed down her pain and held his stare. "I will."

He pressed a kiss to her lips.

And she wondered…could he tell that, this time, she was the one lying?

***

The rough buzz of sound pulled Zander from sleep. His head turned toward the nightstand, and he saw his phone vibrating on the wooden surface. He reached out for it and read the text from Randall quickly.

I'm on the front porch. Need to talk.

Zander cast a quick glance at Alice. Her breathing was slow and easy, and her body was so soft and sweet against his. She'd fallen asleep in his arms. Talk about an act of trust. She might still be furious as hell at him, but deep down, he thought she might be starting to come around. To forgive him, at least, he hoped she was.

He'd meant every word that he'd said to her. Zander would never hurt her again. He couldn't stand to ever see that look of betrayal in her beautiful eyes. The Bureau had been wrong about her. Alice wasn't a perp. She was the victim. And

Zander would all of the power he had to keep her safe.

He pressed a soft kiss to her cheek and then slid from bed. Zander paused long enough to yank on his jeans, and he shoved his phone into the back pocket. He made his way downstairs, his bare feet not making a sound as he avoided the steps that creaked. Once on the main floor, he peeked out of the window, because yeah, it paid to be careful. A killer was on the loose, and he was going to verify the identity of his visitor before he opened the front door.

His partner was on the porch, his hands loose at his sides, the light glaring down at him. Zander unlocked the door and ushered him inside.

"Got fucking news," Randall muttered, face tight.

Zander locked the door. "And the news *isn't* that you caught the bastard?"

Randall gave a hard, negative shake of his head.

Figured. And the way Randall was acting, this news wasn't going to be good. Zander headed for the den. He cast a quick glance upstairs, but saw no sign of Alice.

"Where is she?" Randall asked him.

"Sleeping. Guilt tore her apart when she found out what happened to Cara." The fire had long gone out, and the charred remains of the wood were cold in the fireplace. He propped his shoulder against the mantel as he faced Randall. "What brought you to my place at 3 a.m.?"

Randall shoved his hands into the pockets of his jeans. "He was watching her."

"Yeah, I suspected as much. He's stalking her, just like his other—"

"No, Z, you don't get me. After Cara—" He broke off, then squared his shoulders. "I brought in a new crime scene team. They went over every inch of Alice May's cabin. And they found what we'd missed before."

Zander tensed. "Just what had we missed?"

"He had cameras in her place. Tiny as hell. Top of the line. He was watching her. In the bedroom. In the bathroom. In the kitchen. He was watching her everywhere she went in that house."

Zander's stomach twisted as rage burned in his blood. "If the cameras were transmitting, our techs can track the signal, they can find—"

"They're trying, but this guy is good. The signal is bouncing around over half of the United States. The guy knew what he was doing."

And Zander understood. "Shit. The power— it went out during the big storm. My cabin went black, and I bet Alice's did, too." Everything made terrible sense. "At my place, the lights were out for a good ten, maybe fifteen minutes." *Dammit, dammit!* "The perp didn't know she'd left. The last thing he saw was probably the footage of her turning out her lights and getting into bed."

Randall nodded. "Then when he went inside and she wasn't there, the guy went berserk."

"He's going to know you found the cameras." If the killer had still been watching, he would have seen the techs make the discovery.

"Yeah, he'll know." Again, Randall gave a grim nod. "Already talked to our profilers. And they say he was watching her as a form of control. He needed to know everything she was doing. Needed to make sure she didn't get close to anyone else. And now that he can't see her, they think he's going to unravel."

Like the bastard wasn't already unhinged? "That's how he knew Cara wasn't Alice. He could see Cara in the cabin. He could see us all. He's been a step ahead of us all along." Zander surged away from the fireplace, every muscle in his body tight. "Dammit!"

"FBI brass wants Alice pulled in. They don't think she's secure here. And the profilers want a run at her. They think she knows this bastard."

Yeah, Zander thought the same thing. Like he'd told Alice, why else would the guy disguise his voice?

Randall raked a hand over his face. "The story is going to make the news. No way to hide it. The town is already buzzing about Cara's death. And as soon as word is out that the Secret Admirer is hunting again, the shit storm will begin. Alice will be hounded by the media every second. She won't be any use to us then."

Zander's hands fisted. "FBI brass wants to move Alice to another safe house because they're still planning to use her as bait. It's not about keeping her away from the media." Not about keeping Alice safe.

"You know how this stuff works, Z." Frustration was clear on Randall's face. "Look, you think I like this? We were all wrong about her. Now the killer is gunning for her. We need to get her moved, and we need to come up with a plan B, fast."

The stairs creaked. Zander's gaze immediately jerked toward them. Alice was there. Her hair was tousled, and she wore his shirt—it fell to her thighs. Her face was pale, and her eyes appeared even bluer than normal as she stared back at him.

Zander exhaled slowly. How much had she heard? *Probably too much.* He cleared his throat and asked Randall, "What about Tiffany? Have you found her?"

"No." Grim. Angry. "But we found video footage of her heading into the hospital's parking garage. She went in, but never came out."

"Any sign of her vehicle?"

"Her car is still in the hospital's garage."

Alice climbed down the last few steps. Her bare toes curled into the hardwood floor. "He has her."

"That's what we believe." Randall wasn't pulling any punches.

Alice glanced down at the floor, then she squared her shoulders. Her chin lifted. "I'm not going to a new safe house."

Oh, hell…Zander stalked toward her. "Alice—"

She lifted her hand, stopping him. "The media will close in, just like you said. But I'm not going to hide from them. I'll give them a statement, one that I know they can deliver to the killer." Her lips twisted in a smile that never reached her eyes. "I'm sure he'll be watching. After all, Randall, I heard you say how much he enjoys watching me."

Zander's hands fisted. "Baby, just take a breath, you don't—"

"I will go on camera, and I'll offer him a deal. Me for Tiffany, just what he wanted." Her voice was flat, almost eerily calm. "And you two—well, I'm hoping the FBI has the best tracking equipment in the world. You can track me when I go to the exchange. You can follow me. You can find him." A little shrug. "And if everything works out the way I hope, I'll get to live."

He couldn't stay away from her. Zander eliminated the last bit of distance between him and Alice. "You don't need to do this."

"But the FBI wants me as bait—"

"Screw that. I can take you away. I can put you in a location he will *never* find." For the first time, he was putting something else before job and duty. He was putting her first.

And Zander had the feeling that for the rest of his life, he would *always* be putting her first.

Alice shook her head. "But if he can't find me, then he'll hurt someone else. He'll kill Tiffany—"

"He may already have," Randall interrupted to say. "We don't know what this bastard is planning. Or what he has already done."

"If she is dead, then he'll just take someone else. He won't stop. Not unless I stop him." Her hand lifted and pressed to Zander's chest. "Either he was working with Hugh all along...or this guy—he got fixated on me *because* of everything that Hugh did. Either way, I'm in this. I don't want to be in it." Her eyes were so deep and beautiful. "I want to be normal. I want a normal life. I want..." Her words trailed away as her lashes swept down.

"Alice?"

After a tense moment, she looked back up at him. Wistfully, she said, "I want to date." Her head cocked to the right. "I want to not be afraid to go out in public. I want to stop feeling like someone is always watching." Her lower lip trembled. "But I guess that wasn't just a feeling, was it? He *was* always watching."

Yes, and Zander wanted to tear the bastard apart.

"I'm not asking you if I can do this." Once again, her words were flat. "I'm telling you. I will give a statement to the media. I will speak to this killer. And then when the time comes, I'm going for the trade." Her hand pressed right over his heart. "But I would sure feel better if you were with me. If you were at my side for the press conference. If you put the tracker on me and you followed me to the trade. Because, see, you told me...you said I could trust you, that I could count on you."

"Fucking always."

"Good." The grimness of her eyes eased just a bit. "I need you."

He wanted to scoop her into his arms. Wanted to get the hell out of there—

"Tiffany Shaw is missing. He has her. I want to get her back." Her gaze pleaded with him. "Help me."

Dammit. "You don't leave my sight. Not for a minute, understand?" And he didn't care if Randall was watching them. Zander kissed her. Hard and deep. "Because, baby, if something happens to you…" No, nothing would happen. He'd see to it. Nothing *could* happen to her.

Alice smiled at him. The smile *did* reach her eyes this time.

And the heart beneath her hands — his heart — it beat faster. Just for her.

Always, for her.

CHAPTER TEN

"You're fucking her, Z."

Zander didn't glance away from the closed ladies' room door. Alice was in there, and in moments, she'd come out to face the crowd. They were at the sheriff's station, reporters were on the front steps, and it was nearly showtime. They'd planned their press conference for one p.m. It was twelve fifty-five.

"You were half-dressed, so was she, and then you kissed her..." Randall's words trailed away. "Don't exactly have to be a super agent to put those pieces together and get the end result."

"I'm not fucking her." He could feel the light weight of his holster. "I'm falling in love with her."

"What?"

"You heard me, man. Not like I stuttered. I'm falling for Alice May, and when this shit is over, I'm going to do my best to get her to fall for *me*, too." He could feel Randall's eyes on him.

"Shit." A quick bark of laughter came from Randall. "You're serious. You — you are caught in that woman's web."

Zander turned his head, just for a moment, and locked eyes with his partner.

Shock slid onto Randall's face. "You...you aren't falling. You *already* fell, didn't you?"

Before he could speak, there was a commotion near the entrance to the station. A tall, dark-haired man rushed inside. "Alice!" His gold gaze darted around frantically.

"Aw, damn, I recognize him," Randall muttered.

A deputy hurried to grab the fellow. "No reporters allowed inside, buddy. You need to wait out there with the rest of them — "

"I'm not a reporter," the man snapped back. "I'm family. Alice May's family, and I need to see her, *now.*"

Zander had stiffened as recognition hit him. He knew the guy charging toward him. And, no, the fellow *wasn't* Alice's family. The guy was Jonathan Collins, and since Alice hadn't gotten the chance to say her "I do" with Jonathan's brother, Hugh, the man was zero relation to her.

Right at that moment, the bathroom door opened. Alice's heels tapped over the floor as she hurried to Zander. "I'm ready," she announced to him, "or as ready as I — *Jonathan?*"

Zander stepped in front of the fellow who *shouldn't* have been in that station. How in the hell had he gotten past the deputies outside of the building? Probably with his BS about being family. Were the guys really that clueless that they'd let the bozo just waltz inside? *Uh, yeah, probably.* "You need to stop right the hell there," Zander flatly informed Jonathan.

Jonathan Collins staggered to a stop, but his gaze darted toward Alice. "Are the stories true?" His voice had gone hoarse. "Is the Secret Admirer killing again? Is he after you?"

Randall closed in on the fellow. "Mr. Collins, I'm going to frisk you."

Jonathan's eyes widened. "What? Why in the hell —"

"To make sure you don't have a weapon on you. To make sure that you are not a threat to Alice May or anyone else in this station."

"I would *never* be a threat to Alice!" Jonathan's face flushed red. "But go ahead, pat me down. I don't have anything to hide. I'm here because I'm worried. I'm scared as all hell for Alice."

Randall's patdown was swift but thorough. "He's clean."

"Of course, I am," Jonathan huffed. "I'm not some criminal, I'm not —"

"Your brother?" Zander supplied.

Jonathan's chin notched up. "If the Secret Admirer is hunting again, then don't you all see? Don't you finally understand? You were wrong about Hugh. It was never him! That's what I told the reporters, time and time again. My brother was set up! He didn't—"

Alice moved to Zander's side. Her sweet scent surrounded him. When she took a step toward Jonathan, Zander's hand flew out and curled around her wrist. He gave a quick, negative shake of his head. There was no way he was letting her get closer to that guy. "Are you forgetting something?" Zander drawled to Jonathan. "Like, oh, I don't know…the dead body that was in the back of your brother's vehicle?"

The red faded from Jonathan's cheeks. Now, he looked too pale. "I knew my brother. He wasn't a killer. Someone framed him, the same someone I heard about on the news first thing this morning. That's why I hauled ass to get here. *The real killer is here.* Unless you think a dead man is hunting Alice."

"No." Zander gave Jonathan a cold smile. "I know our perp is very much alive."

Jonathan's hands fisted and unfisted as he focused on Alice. "You should have called me. At the first sign of trouble, you should have called me. You and I—we're family. We're the only—"

"You're not family," Zander cut in flatly.

Jonathan's brow furrowed as his gaze swung to Zander. His gaze dropped, falling to Zander's hand as it wrapped around Alice's wrist. The furrow deepened, and then he was studying Zander's face. "Who are you?"

The man who will stand beside Alice for the rest of her life, if she'll have me.

But it was Alice who answered, "He's Special Agent Zander Todd. He's after the man who — who has been targeting me."

Right then, the station doors opened again. A female agent with dark red hair entered and inclined her head toward Zander. "We're ready," Kristy Law announced.

Show time. Zander glanced down at Alice. "Are you sure? You can still back out." *I can still get you the hell out of here.*

But she nodded. "Just stay with me."

Like she had to ask. "Always."

She rewarded him with a quick smile, then her gaze slid to Jonathan. "We'll talk after the press conference, okay? I'll explain things, but I have to go now."

Jonathan's jaw clenched, but he nodded.

Zander fired a fast, hard glance at Randall. He knew his partner would get the message. *Don't take your eyes off that sonofabitch.* Because Jonathan Collins being right there...oh, yeah, that looked suspicious as shit. One brother had been a sadistic killer.

Was the other brother just like him?

They were about to find out.

Zander's hand slid down. Alice's fingers curled around his, and together, they walked to the station doors. He could see the swarm of reporters waiting outside. A podium had been set up in front of the station. The microphone was ready. So were the cameras.

He heard Alice pull in a deep breath. And then the deputies opened the doors.

The reporters surged forward.

"Alice May — is it true that the Secret Admirer is hunting you?"

***

"What in the hell is happening?" Jonathan Collins glared at the station's front doors. "Why is she talking to the reporters? Alice *never* talked to them before."

Randall swept his gaze over the fellow. Jonathan Collins wasn't quite as tall as his brother had been. His shoulders were a little thinner than Hugh's. But the guy was still strong and lean. And he'd sure gotten to the little town of Sky fast. Very, very fast.

Jonathan's head turned as he pinned Randall with an angry stare. "Is the FBI making her do this?"

Randall's lips quirked. "No, I've figured out that no one can make Alice do anything. It's all her choice." He pointed toward the glass doors. "Alice wants to talk to the killer. She wants to speak directly to him, and this is her way."

"This is fucking insane! On the news — the reporters were already saying she'd been targeted! That an FBI agent who looked like Alice had been killed!"

Randall didn't speak.

Jonathan's hand shook as he raked it through his hair. "Does Alice have a death wish?"

Randall might have wondered the same thing, at first. But then he'd realized — Alice just wanted the nightmare to end. "We believe the Secret Admirer has taken a victim, a woman named Tiffany Shaw. Alice wants to get that woman back."

Jonathan's eyes squeezed shut. "I heard that part on the freaking news, too." After a tense moment of silence, his eyes opened. "And you know what? There's no need to bullshit. If the Secret Admirer has that woman — if the *real* killer has her — she's already dead. Alice won't get anything back but a corpse."

Randall had read all of the interview notes on Jonathan Collins. The guy had been singing the same song about Hugh Collins from day one — Jonathan believed his brother had been framed. "I'm Special Agent Randall Cane." It was past time for an official introduction. "I'm working this case with Agent Todd. If you have any relevant information to provide to us—"

"My brother wasn't a killer."

Same song. "A woman's body was in his vehicle. It's pretty hard to overlook the evidence, don't you think?"

"Not if he was framed."

Some people just couldn't see the truth.

"Someone could have dumped that woman's body in Hugh's SUV. Hugh wasn't even routinely using that vehicle! It had sat in his garage for months because he preferred to use his motorcycle. The real killer could have known that, he could have—" But Jonathan broke off. "Why am I even wasting my breath? You have to see the truth now. The Secret Admirer is hunting again, and if we aren't careful, he's going to kill Alice." Jonathan's index finger stabbed into the air. "I'm not letting that happen. Not fucking letting it happen!" He hurried toward the station's entrance, shoved open the glass doors, and rushed outside.

***

A swirl of faces stared back at Alice. Men and women. All shouting questions. She didn't try to answer their questions. Instead, Alice eased out a quick breath as she stared straight ahead. She leaned toward the microphone. "Come after me."

The questions stopped. She wasn't there to speak to the reporters. She was there to speak to *him.*

"The victims have all been *me.* Haven't they?" She didn't need profilers to tell her that part. "My hair. My face shape. My eyes." Her heart felt as if it were about to burst out of her chest. "Only they aren't me. When you hurt them, you don't hurt me." A lie. Their pain hurt her. More guilt. More rage. "If I'm the one you want, if I'm the one you've always been after, then come after me."

Questions fired at her.

Alice shook her head. She felt Zander slip closer to her. Another deep breath, and then... "You have a victim, don't you? Someone else you took. Don't hurt her. I'll make the trade that you offered. Just call me. Tell me when. Tell me where. I will come. I will do whatever you want. It's time, don't you think? Time for us to get together. No one else. Just us."

The reporters were screaming.

But Alice was done.

She turned toward Zander. "Get me out of here."

He immediately nodded and took her arm. As they turned from the podium, she saw Jonathan rushing out of the station. The sun hit his close-cropped, dark hair, and for a moment, he looked so much like Hugh.

Hugh…with his laughing eyes. His quick smile.

Hugh…the killer. The liar.

Her chest *hurt*.

Zander didn't take her back inside the station. That wasn't part of the plan. Instead, he led her toward a black SUV that waited near the curb. Another agent held the rear door open for them. Alice jumped inside. "I need to talk with Jonathan. I saw him back there—I need to explain things!"

Zander climbed in with her and slammed the door shut. "We'll contact him soon. Hell, I'll get a team to bring him to the cabin, okay?" Zander looked toward the front seat. The driver was already in place. "Get us the hell out of here."

The SUV shot away from the curb—and the crowd. Alice glanced back. The cameras were still rolling. Jonathan had moved onto the sidewalk, and he gazed after her with a tight, angry expression.

Alice fumbled and pulled her phone from her pocket. The FBI agents could track every call that she received. She just *had* to get the call when it came in. Then they could act. Then they could move. "The killer is going to call," Alice whispered.

Zander's fingers curled under her chin, and he turned her head toward him. She gazed at him, getting lost just for a moment in the darkness of his stare.

"I will be at your side," Zander promised her. "Every second, you understand?"

She wasn't going to argue with that. She wanted him close. "I think I'd like a gun."

"Hell, yes, you're getting a gun."

She swallowed to ease the dryness in her throat. "Did I...do okay?"

Zander kissed her. A soft, tender kiss. "You did better than okay. You hit all the right buttons, covered it just the way the profilers predicted would draw the perp in." Another kiss. "Baby, you are perfect."

Perfect. A shiver slid over her. "No," Alice told him with utter certainty. "That's something I'm not."

CHAPTER ELEVEN

"What in the hell are you doing, Alice?" Jonathan demanded.

Alice glanced up from her position on the couch. They were at Zander's cabin. They'd been there since the press conference, and now, as the sun dipped beneath the horizon, she had to face-off with Jonathan. Randall had just brought Jonathan to the cabin. She'd asked for the meeting with him. She'd needed him to understand—

"I have to do this," Alice told him. "A woman is missing—"

"She could already be dead." Jonathan shook his head. "You know once he actually took them, the Secret Admirer immediately started to torture his victims."

Because he attacked in a frenzy. A slow buildup of stalking, of thinking that his victim was perfect and then finding out...

She wasn't.

Zander sat right beside Alice. "The profilers all said the original Secret Admirer went into a rage when the objects of his desire did something to upset him. That's why the attacks were so brutal. But we aren't dealing with the original—"

"Yes, you are!" Jonathan argued fiercely.

Randall's lips thinned as he stood near the fireplace. "We don't know what this perp is going to do. His MO is different. He shot Agent McCoy. So we have no fucking clue what he could be doing to Tiffany Shaw."

"And until we have a body," Zander rose, slowly uncurling his body, "then we work under the assumption that Tiffany is still alive. We have agents, deputies, and volunteers scouring the area for her. We know the killer is still close, so that means that Tiffany has to be close, too."

"How do you know that?" Jonathan immediately demanded.

Zander's stare lingered on Alice. "Because he doesn't have what he wants yet."

Me.

Jonathan's chest rose and fell with his rapid breathing. "Alice," Jonathan said her name roughly, pulling her attention to him. "Why didn't you tell me you were going to do this?"

Why? Now Alice also rose. She'd been waiting all afternoon for a call that hadn't come, and as more time passed, her nerves had been shot to hell. "We haven't talked in months."

"Alice, I—"

"Hugh was guilty, Jonathan. Guilty! There was no denying the evidence." But Jonathan had been adamant, and she hadn't been able to stay around him. Every time they'd spoken, he'd argued for Hugh's innocence. He'd demanded that they hunt the real killer. "A body was in the back of the SUV."

Jonathan's lips parted, but he didn't speak.

"I didn't really know Hugh. You didn't really know him. Hugh only showed us what he *wanted* us to see." The perfect fiancé. The loving brother. The charmer. "I stopped talking to you because you still weren't ready to see the truth, but it was a truth I *had* to see." In order to stay sane. In order to get her life back. "Hugh is dead. This guy—whoever he is—he's still out there. And he's not going to get away. The FBI is helping me. We're working together. They'll keep me safe, and they'll stop him."

Jonathan's gaze raked her. "With what? A wire? A GPS monitor? You think that will keep you safe?"

Before she could answer him, her phone rang. She jumped. So did Jonathan. Zander and Randall didn't move.

The phone was on the coffee table. She'd put it there because she wanted it close. She'd pretty much been holding it for hours, and she'd only put it down when Jonathan arrived at the cabin. Now she leaned forward to see—

Unknown Caller. "It's him." It had to be. Didn't it?

Zander's hand closed around her shoulder. "Put him on speaker. The techs will do the rest."

Right. Right. Okay. Sweat covered her as she swiped her finger over the screen. "Hello."

"I saw you on the news," blasted the robotic voice. The exact same voice she'd heard before. "You want to be with me."

"I want you to let Tiffany go. I want to trade places with her."

Robotic laughter. "Are you sure?" And then...

A woman's scream.

Tiffany.

Still alive. Oh, thank God, still alive. "Don't hurt her!" Alice cried out. "Just—just tell me where to meet you. I'll come, I'll be there, I'll—"

"Alone, Alice. You come to me alone. No FBI. No deputies. They don't track you. They don't follow. You come to me."

She was nodding but, of course, he couldn't see that. "Where? When?"

"Now, Alice. Come to me right *now*."

She couldn't pull in deep enough breaths.

"There's an old cemetery at the edge of town. You go there. You walk in alone. I'll find you."

"But—"

"If your lover comes with you, if anyone else is there, I'll put my knife in Tiffany's heart."

The call went dead.

For a moment, all Alice could hear was the sound of her heartbeat. Then...

"Tell me you triangulated the signal." Zander's voice. Strong. Hard.

Her attention snapped toward him. His phone was pressed to his ear. He nodded and said, "Right. Hell, yes, we're putting the tracker on her. And I'll be at that fucking cemetery." He ended the call and shoved the phone into his pocket. He glanced at Randall. "Let's get her wired. The call came from *in* town, less than a mile from the cemetery. The bastard is out there, and we're getting him."

"No!" Jonathan's sharp voice. "You can't do this, Alice! You're going to die!"

Zander snarled, "Time for you to get the fuck out of here." He grabbed Jonathan and guided/shoved the other man toward the door. "Alice will stay safe. You can count on it."

"Because you're going to be with her?" Jonathan sneered at him. "But didn't you hear what that bastard said? He'll kill that other woman—"

"He won't know I'm there." Zander yanked open the door. Alice could see a red-haired deputy outside on the narrow porch. Zander called, "Deputy Ross, Take Mr. Collins to his motel—"

"I can get there my damn self!" Jonathan huffed. He twisted, and Alice saw him crane his neck until he caught sight of her. "Alice, don't do this. I'm begging you."

Didn't he understand? "I have to help her."

Jonathan shook his head. "It's going to be your funeral." He stormed away.

Zander slammed the door shut. His gaze swept over her, softened. "Baby—"

"I have to help her," Alice said again. "Now, where in the hell is the gun I was promised?"

***

"Is the bulletproof vest necessary?" Alice asked as she tugged at the vest Zander had forced her to wear. They were in the back of the SUV—the FBI seemed to have a ton of the dark-colored vehicles—and parked about forty yards from the entrance to the cemetery.

"Yes, it's fucking necessary. The guy shot Cara, and he's not going to get the chance to go for your heart." He pushed the gun into her hand. "Aim and shoot, baby."

"I know how to use a gun." And if the bastard attacked, she wasn't going to hesitate. "Is the tracker working?" The thing had been practically miniscule. The agents didn't think that the killer was actually going to just be standing in the cemetery. They thought he'd be watching her from a distance, that he'd call her and direct her to another location. But the agents were going to be ready for that move.

They were going to be watching. Always.

At least, that was what Alice had been told.

Zander pressed a hand to his earpiece. Then he nodded. "They say it's working perfectly."

Because the device could give GPS coordinates *and* it would transmit every sound it heard. A clever bit of FBI protection.

"I'm going to be close," Zander assured her.

Alice bit her lip. "If you're too close, he'll see you."

"Baby, I was a Ranger for four years. The guy *won't* see me."

Despite everything, she smiled at him. "Thanks for being with me." She was so scared that her fingers were shaking, but having Zander there—she just felt better.

"Where the hell else would I be?" He took her hand. Brought it to his lips. Pressed a kiss to her knuckles. "We're going to take him down. It's going to end tonight."

She kissed him. Brought her mouth to his and kissed him wildly, passionately. "I'm glad I met you."

"Baby—"

"And I get it—okay? The lies. I don't like them. I hate them, in fact, but life is kinda too short for bitterness, and whatever happens next, I don't want you thinking..." Her words were tumbling out, too fast, but she couldn't stop. "I'm not holding on to any anger. I understand. And I'd do it all over again. Eat the sweets you brought to me. Have dinner at my place. Run to you in a rainstorm." She swallowed. "I would always run to you." Alice had to get those words out.

Because she was afraid there might not be another chance to say them.

"And you asked if I would date you...if this craziness was all over, yes, yes, I would date you. And I'd probably love you."

His face tensed. "That's good, sweetheart." His lips feathered over hers. "Because I already do love you."

What?

"And you're going to be fine. You're going to come back to me. And you'll never be afraid of anyone or anything again." He smiled at her, and his smile almost broke her heart. "Because I'm going to spend every day of my life making sure of that fact. I'm going to spend every single day working to make you so happy that there isn't room for fear or doubt."

Randall cleared his throat—from the front seat. He'd driven them to the drop-off spot. "This is some really romantic shit and all..." He coughed. "But, Alice, you need to get moving."

She kissed Zander again. *Not the last time.*
This is not the last time I will kiss him.

"I'll be right there, baby," Zander promised
her gruffly. "You won't see me. But I'll be there."

She nodded. Then she opened the door, and
she did exactly as Randall had said.

She got moving. And Alice also kept a very,
very tight grip on her gun.

***

"She's going to be all right," Randall said as
soon as Alice left the vehicle.

Zander grunted as he yanked on his own
bulletproof vest. "Hell, yes, she is." He inclined
his head to Randall. "Keep a lock on her signal.
Keep talking in my ear. I'm going after her."
Without another word, he slipped out of the
SUV. But unlike Alice, Zander didn't walk
straight toward the old, sagging cemetery gates.
Instead, he headed for the shadows. He'd learned
to blend as a Ranger. Learned to enter a scene
without a sound. Learned silence and the fine art
of camouflage. He'd watch Alice. He'd stay close.

Because there was no way he'd lose the
woman he loved. Those words hadn't been some
lie. He'd never lie to her again. Alice owned his
heart, and he would keep her safe.

I'm watching, baby. I've got your back.

***

She'd never liked cemeteries. The headstones gleamed in the moonlight, and Alice found herself walking around them carefully. As a kid, when she'd visited her grandfather's grave, she'd always been so afraid that she'd step on the dead. She'd imagined the bodies beneath the ground, and it had seemed so wrong to just walk across someone that way. So she still walked through the cemetery as if she were that eight-year-old girl, carefully creeping around the headstones and hunching her shoulders against the wind that howled around her. Her jacket covered the bullet-proof vest that she wore, and it gave her a bit of warmth on that surprisingly cold, spring night.

Her phone rang, jarring her. Her right hand gripped the gun, but her left shoved into her pocket and pulled out her phone.

Unknown caller. Zander and the other agents had predicted she'd get a call from the perp as soon as she got inside the cemetery. The FBI had been right. She answered the phone, fully expecting to hear that robotic voice filling her ear—

"Get rid of the tracker or he'll kill me!"

That wasn't a robotic voice. It was the hushed, desperate gasp of a terrified woman.

"Tiffany?" Alice gasped.

"Yes, oh, God, it's me! Get rid of the tracker. Do you hear me? You have to get rid of it! Now!

The FBI gave you a tracker. He can see you. He's watching. Take it out. Crush it beneath your shoe. Please," Tiffany begged, her hoarse whisper almost painful to hear. "God, please, get rid of it—he's hurting me!"

Shit. *Shit.* Alice yanked out the small tracking device. She crushed it beneath her shoe, grinding it into the hard earth. "It's gone! Okay? It's gone!"

Silence.

Her fingers clenched around the phone.

"Now the gun," Tiffany whispered. "You have to get rid of the gun now. He can see it." No more screams. Just a rough, muffled plea.

Alice didn't put down the gun.

"He sees you. He's always watching," Tiffany continued, voice husky with tears. "He has a knife at my throat right now, and I can feel it cutting me. Please…please…put the gun down. Just put it on the headstone beside you."

But Alice hesitated. If the perp had a knife at Tiffany's throat, and if he was watching… "You're here, aren't you?" In the cemetery. The perp wasn't going to lure her to another location, like the FBI suspected. The perp *was* there. The FBI was supposed to be watching the cemetery from all angles. They'd thought for sure that she would be taken to another location.

But they'd been wrong. The killer was there. He was inside with her.

"The gun, Alice!" Tiffany's voice broke. "Put it down, he's—ah, he's hurting me!"

Dammit. Alice put down the gun. She lifted her right hand in the air, showing that she wasn't armed any longer. Her tracking device was gone, but the FBI was still monitoring her phone. They'd hear everything that was being said. They'd rush inside.

"Now walk forward," Tiffany told her, voice low and thin. "He says...F-forward twenty feet. Turn at the broken angel. D-don't pick up your gun. H-he'll kill me..." Her breath heaved out. "And drop your phone. He says...l-leave it there..." The call ended.

"I hope to hell you got all of that," Alice muttered. The FBI had better have gotten that. She dropped her phone onto the ground and hurried forward. Twenty feet? She wasn't sure where—

The broken angel. Beneath the moonlight, she saw the statue. The wings had fallen away, and the angel seemed to be grieving as he looked down into...an open grave.

A large hole had been dug into the earth. The hole was the perfect size for a coffin. A deep and wide hole, one that disappeared far below. Alice stopped right near that massive opening, her gaze sliding into the darkness that waited below.

Footsteps rushed toward her. Alice spun around just as Tiffany appeared from the darkness. The woman's face was twisted and desperate, and she hurtled right at Alice. Alice reached out her hands, trying to grab for the other woman—

And Tiffany shoved Alice. Shoved her hard, and Alice slipped on the loose dirt. She tumbled back, falling into the gaping hole. Falling right into the open grave that waited for her. Alice hit hard, landing on her back, and the wind was knocked from her lungs. For a moment, she didn't move, a moment that seemed to last forever. Then Alice looked up.

Tiffany stood on the edge of the open grave. She had a gun in her hand. "Hello, bitch," Tiffany told her, triumph thick in her voice. "You're finally where you belong."

***

"Close in!" Zander snarled into the headpiece. "Fucking swarm, now. He's in the cemetery. Get agents inside!" Zander didn't hesitate. He hurtled over the old fence and landed easily on the other side. Alice's phone call had been fed into his listening device, and he'd never been more grateful for the techs that worked at the FBI. He rushed through the darkness, looking for the broken angel. And it was right there. Up ahead. He could see it—

He advanced without a sound, his gun up and ready. *I'm here, Alice.*

A dark-haired woman stood a few feet away. She lifted a gun and aimed into what looked like an open grave. The wind blew her hair back —

Not Alice. Not my Alice!

"Stop!" Zander yelled. "FBI!"

She didn't stop. She fired. The blast echoed around him.

He bellowed, "Drop the weapon! Drop it fucking *now!*"

Laughing, she spun toward him. *Tiffany Shaw.* "Too late!" She didn't drop the weapon. She pointed it at him. "She's gone. Dead in the grave, just like he is."

No, dammit, no!

"She never deserved him. Alice wasn't perfect. Alice wasn't good enough. She didn't appreciate him." The moonlight showed Tiffany's features so clearly — she was smiling. "I read the stories. Realized the Secret Admirer was looking for me. *Me.* I'm the woman he always wanted. I have the dark hair. I have the blue eyes. I'm perfect. Perfect for him. Alice was just in the way. So I put her where she belonged." Tiffany took a step forward. "Alice is in the ground. Dead in the grave." Tiffany's voice took on a sing-song quality. "Alice is in the ground. Dead in the —"

"Drop the fucking gun, or I will shoot you." Fear had iced Zander's veins. Alice couldn't be dead. Hell, no.

But Tiffany shook her head. "No, how about I shoot—" Her words ended in a scream because someone had just grabbed Tiffany. Hands had shot out of the open grave. Hands that locked around Tiffany's ankles and yanked her, hard. Tiffany twisted and slammed face-first into the ground. Then she rolled, screaming, and she crawled for the grave, trying to aim her gun again, trying to shoot into that hole—

Trying to shoot at Alice.

"Stop!" Zander yelled.

Tiffany didn't.

So he fired. The bullet blasted into Tiffany's back. She'd just shoved to her knees as she took aim, and the bullet plunged into her. She let out another scream, and her upper body spun toward him as she took aim at Zander—

He fired again. A shot to her chest. Her eyes bulged. She gasped. Shuddered.

Then she fell. Her body sagged back, then slipped right into the open grave.

Zander ran forward. He could hear the frantic rush of footsteps as the other agents closed in. "Alice!" Zander roared her name. He fell to his knees at the edge of the open grave, his gaze flying below—

Tiffany was in the grave. Bleeding. Twitching. And Alice was crouched beside her. Alice's hand was on Tiffany's cheek. It looked like Tiffany was talking.

Zander jumped into the grave.

"I-I...was...p-perfect..." Tiffany's voice slurred.

Alice shook her head. "No one is perfect."

But Tiffany didn't hear her. Because Tiffany Shaw—

She was dead. Her eyes had sagged shut, and her body had gone still. Zander put his hand to Tiffany's throat, just to be sure. No pulse.

"She wasn't a victim." Alice's soft voice.

He caught her hand in his. Lifted her up. "Baby, I saw her shoot—I thought she'd killed you!"

Alice was still staring at Tiffany's face. "Bulletproof vest. She knew I had the tracker on me, but she didn't know about the vest." She rubbed her chest. "Hurts like hell, but I'm okay—"

He yanked her into his arms. Crushed her against him. Held her as tight as he could.

"I don't want to be in a grave," Alice whispered. "Please, get me the hell out of here. I managed to jump up and grab her legs, but I couldn't get out."

He pulled back so he could stare at her beautiful face.

A tear slid down her cheek. "I don't want to be in a grave," she said again, voice ragged.

He lifted her up. "Randall!" Zander yelled. "Get Alice's arms!"

And his partner was there. His partner, four other agents, some deputies — they'd all come running. They'd all been ready to take out the Secret Admirer.

Randall caught Alice's arms and lifted her out of the grave.

"She wasn't the victim," Alice said again, her words drifting back to Zander. "I thought...I was helping her. But Tiffany — it was her. Her all along."

Zander glanced down at the body once more. Tiffany Shaw's eyes were closed, but it sure as hell looked as if a faint smile curled her lips.

CHAPTER TWELVE

"A crime scene team made an interesting discovery at Tiffany Shaw's place." Zander paced around the small conference room at the sheriff's station. "I had a hunch, and they followed up on it...The woman was wild for the Secret Admirer, so I thought she might be imitating him in other ways." And he'd been right. "There was a loose floorboard in her bedroom closet." Just like there had been one in Alice's closet. "When they pulled it up..." He pointed to the evidence bags on the table. "They found that shit."

Newspaper clippings. Magazine stories. Tales that seemed to glamourize all of the Secret Admirer's kills.

"She was obsessed," Randall added. He sat in one of the chairs near the small table, a line of shadow covering his jaw. "She got hooked on the killer. I'm sure the shrinks will say she developed some fancy disorder or had some dissociative episode, but the truth is—"

"She was a killer." Alice's voice was flat. Her cheeks were too pale, and her grip on the cup of coffee in front of her seemed too tight. Alice's gaze darted to Zander. "She killed Cara McCoy, didn't she?"

He nodded. "We're waiting for a ballistics match, but…" He yanked a hand over his face. "Tiffany had a bag stashed near the grave she'd dug at the cemetery. We found a rifle in that bag. Same type of gun, same type of bullet used at your cabin, so yeah, I think she killed Cara."

"And Julianna Stiles," Randall added with a sad sigh. "Because we found a picture of Julianna shoved in with all of the newspaper clippings that Tiffany had in her closet."

Alice shook her head. "Why? Why kill Julianna? Why come after me? Why do *any* of this?"

Zander knew Randall was right. The shrinks would come up with a reason. An explanation as to how and why the woman's life had broken apart and she'd turned to murder, but from where Zander was standing…from what he'd seen with other cases… "When Randall said she was obsessed, he's right. We've seen others get obsessed with killers. Tiffany Shaw was fixated. She knew the Secret Admirer was looking for perfection, and she wanted to be his perfect match. And if she was going to be that person…"

"Then Julianna had to die," Randall muttered.

"Because she had dark hair and blue eyes?" Alice asked, her lower lip trembling.

"Because she was a test. A practice run." That was what Zander thought, anyway, and he hated to say it, but—

Alice's eyes widened. "Julianna was a practice kill...because Tiffany was working her way up to me?"

Yes.

Her shoulders slumped. "Can I go home now? Is it all over?"

No, it was far from over. There was a shit ton of evidence to still collect and bag from Tiffany's home and from the cemetery. There were reports to write. People to interview—people who'd lived near Tiffany. People who'd worked with her at the hospital. She was dead, but the case wasn't closed, not yet.

"I'm so tired," Alice added. And she looked it. Exhausted.

He hurried to her and put his hand on her shoulder. "I'll get a deputy to take you back to our place." *Our place.* It wasn't, but saying the words felt right. He could imagine having a place with Alice. He could imagine a whole life with her.

Maybe now, they'd get that chance.

"Thank you." Her hand rose and curled over his. "For everything, Zander—just, thank you."

Her gaze held his. "I didn't want you to kill for me. I never wanted that."

There was so much he wanted to say to Alice, but his partner was watching every damn thing. Zander turned his head and glared at Randall.

Randall blinked. "Hey, um, you know what? I think I need to check on some files. Right now." He saluted and hurried from the room. The door closed behind him with a soft click.

Then Zander did what he'd been aching to do. He pulled Alice out of the chair and into his arms. He buried his face in her hair, and he just held her.

She'd been shot. The vest had stopped the bullet, but his Alice had one hell of a bruise. The EMTs on scene had checked her out while he'd watched, unable to leave her side. Too fucking scared to leave her.

"You don't get shot again," he told her gruffly, as he finally forced his head to lift. "You don't stalk into cemeteries at night, and you sure as hell don't put your gun down before a face-off with a killer."

Her head cocked to the side. "She was so believable on the phone. I thought the killer had her. That he was going to hurt her." A faint line appeared between her eyebrows. "All of those phone calls—they were really always her? Because I could have sworn..." Her words trailed away.

"It makes sense," Zander told her because he'd thought about this, too. "She used the voice distorter because she didn't want you to know you were talking with a woman. She used the gun on Cara, used the stolen sedan to come after you — all of that was different from the original Secret Admirer." His lips curled down. "She was a disturbed woman, Alice. But she's gone, and she will never hurt anyone else again."

Alice shivered. "Why doesn't it feel over then?"

Because she'd lived with fear and pain for too long. Because he knew she'd spent the last year always looking over her shoulder. Always waiting for something else to happen. "Where do you want to go?" Zander asked, trying to distract her. Just wanting to make some of the shadows leave her eyes.

"Go?" She blinked. "I-I thought you were getting a deputy to take me home — "

"I mean on our date. You did promise we'd date, right? So you pick the place. Any place you want, I'll take you there." *Baby, I'll take you anywhere. I'll give you anything.*

Her lips curved a little bit, even if the smile never reached her eyes. "A promise is a promise."

"Damn straight it is." He had no intention of letting Alice go. He was about to begin the biggest operation of his life — getting her to stay with him. Forever. Because he didn't want anything less from her. Zander kissed her. A slow and tender kiss. Unfortunately, when he kissed Alice, things never stayed slow. They got hot. Fast. And he got hungry for her. "Go home," he rasped against her mouth. "Soak in a hot bath. Relax. And I'll be there as soon as I can."

Her hands pressed to his chest. "I'll go home, but I'll wait on that soak...until you can join me."

The woman knew exactly how to twist him up. Zander walked her out of the conference room. Their fingers twined together. They headed toward the general area of the station —

"Alice!" Jonathan jumped up from his chair as soon as he saw her. He rushed forward and pulled her into a big, tight hug. "Oh, God, is it true? That woman — she faked her own kidnapping? She tried to *kill* you?"

Zander sure as shit didn't like the way the guy clung so tightly to Alice, but he was trying to keep his cool.

Alice pushed against Jonathan's body, easing out of his hold. "It's true." Her voice was brittle, and she was still far too pale. "She's...she's dead, though, Jon. Before she could shoot at me again, Zander stopped her."

Jonathan's gaze flew to Zander. The other man stiffened but inclined his head as he said, "Thank you, Agent Todd. Alice is the only family I've got left. I couldn't lose her."

"I'm okay," Alice told him quietly. "Just…I'm exhausted. I want to get out of here before the reporters start attacking."

Face grim, Jonathan told her, "They're lined up out front. I had to fight my way past them to get in the station."

Zander motioned to the avidly watching deputy. A familiar fellow with bright, red hair. "Deputy Ross, I want you to take Alice back to my cabin—"

"I'll take her!" Jonathan immediately offered. "The reporters will swarm on any official vehicle that leaves this place." He slanted a fast glance at Alice. "I'll move my car around to the back. You can slip out that way, and I'll take you to the cabin."

Zander tensed. "That's not necessary. The deputy—"

Jonathan's chin lifted. "I'm not my brother. I get it—you don't trust me. Not one bit. But I'm not Hugh. And, shit, he wasn't the man I thought, okay? I'm dealing with that the best I can. He was a monster. I didn't want to see it, but that's what he was."

"It's nothing personal," Zander told him. And it wasn't. This was about Alice's safety. Her safety came before everything else. "But until this case is officially closed, I want Alice to have either a deputy or an agent keeping watch on her."

Alice's eyes widened. "But—"

"There are a few questions left. Just a few." He also couldn't shake the knot of fear in his gut. He pointed to the deputy. "Deputy Greg Ross will take you to the cabin. He'll stay with you until I get there."

A muscle flexed in Jonathan's jaw. "Then I'll be following them because…" Now he turned to look at Alice. "We need to talk. To *really* talk. It's been too long. And I just—you're right. I need to stop pretending and face the past." He straightened his spine. "Hugh Collins was a murderer. He killed six women."

"Five," Randall corrected as he approached their group. "Your brother killed five women."

Jonathan blinked. "Five?" He shook his head. "That's right. Just five."

The deputy had collected his keys. He nodded to Alice. "You ready, Ms. May?"

"Yes." Her gaze lingered on Zander. "I'll see you soon."

Zander pulled her into a hug. "Hell, yes, you will." He held her a moment, then let her go. "Take her out the back," he told the deputy. "I'll go address the reporters and keep them busy so you can slip away."

He watched as the deputy led her away. Then he took a step toward the station's entrance.

But Jonathan moved into his path. "You…love her?"

He wasn't going to deny that. He'd never deny Alice. "Yes."

Anger flashed in Jonathan's gaze. "You lied to her. You tricked her, and you think you get her now? You think that is how things will work out for you?"

"I think it's not any of your business." He gave Jonathan a cold smile. "Now, excuse me. I have reporters waiting." Because if he didn't distract them, they might find Alice. So he marched for the front glass doors. He shoved them open. Raised his hands. "The FBI would like to make an official statement..."

Immediately, the reporters rushed toward him.

***

"I'll be right outside if you need me, Ms. May," Deputy Ross said as he ducked his head and shoved his hands into his pockets.

They'd gotten out to the cabin without attracting the attention of the reporters. Thanks to Zander. He'd provided the perfect distraction for their getaway. The reporters had been so eager to hear a new update now that the killer had been stopped. Sure, like Zander had said, there were still some loose ends, but as far as the Press was concerned, Alice knew they'd consider the case closed.

Over.

So why didn't it feel that way to her?

"There he is," the deputy added as Jonathan's car turned onto the cabin's long, winding drive. His headlights cut through the darkness. "You sure you want to see him?"

They were overdue for this talk. It was time to put this particular part of her past to rest. "Yes, I'm sure." So she waited on the steps as Jonathan parked and exited his car. He hurried toward her, and the light from the porch spilled onto him.

So far, it had really been one hell of a night.

She rubbed the bruise on her chest, the one she'd gotten courtesy of Tiffany's bullet. The bruise ached, but she'd take a bruise any day over what might have been.

When Jonathan approached the porch, she opened the cabin's front door. "Come inside." She had the feeling this would be the last time they talked for a while. He was part of her past, but Zander was going to be her future. Alice glanced at the deputy. "Are you sure you're okay out here?" She hated to leave him just standing in the dark.

"Got orders, ma'am. I keep watch until Agent Todd arrives."

"You can come inside—"

"No, thank you." He gave her a quick smile. "Can't watch the perimeter as well if I'm in there."

"The danger is over," Jonathan said, climbing the wooden steps. "Alice is safe now. You should be able to return to town."

But Deputy Greg Ross shook his head. "Like I said, I've got my orders." He gave Alice a quick smile. "I'll be out here if you need me."

"She's safe now," Jonathan spoke quickly. "There's nothing to worry about."

It almost sounded as if he were trying to reassure himself of that fact.

A few moments later, she and Jonathan were in the den, near the fireplace. The deputy had taken up his position outside. Alice didn't sit on the couch. She stood, with her arms wrapped around her stomach, and faced the man who would have been her brother-in-law. If things hadn't gone so horribly wrong.

Jonathan waited a small distance away from her. A dark line of stubble covered his jaw. His shoulders slumped as he stared at Alice, and then he cut right to the chase. "I've gone over things in my head a million times. Hugh and I grew up in the same house. Lived almost the same life. But how could one of us end up normal, one never breaking a law, following every rule, and the other…" He swallowed. "How did the other end up so different?"

Alice didn't speak. She understood that he needed to get this off his chest.

"Our father—he was such an asshole. Nothing was ever good enough. Nothing could please him. Demand, demand, demand—that's all he ever did. I tried to protect Hugh from him. I swear, I did. But I guess I didn't try hard enough."

"Hugh...he didn't remember his dad." Because he'd died when Hugh was just a little kid.

"That's what he said, huh?" Jonathan exhaled. "I remember him too well. When the bastard passed, our mom tried to make things right. She gave us everything. *Everything*. Until the day she died." His head tipped forward. "So how did it happen? How did one brother become so fucked up?" His hands fisted at his sides. "That poor dead woman. What was her name? Tiffany something? She was deluded, wasn't she? Thinking she was going to kill you."

Alice remembered staring at Tiffany's still body. "I didn't want her to wind up dead. I wanted to save her."

But Jonathan shook his head. "You just can't save some people." His jaw hardened. "And the FBI agent made sure of that, didn't he? He was the one who fired the shot. He was the one who killed her, not you, Alice. Never you." Jonathan took a step toward her. His gaze had softened. "Because you can't kill another person. It's just not in you. You're too kind. Too good." Another step. His hand lifted and the back of his fingers brushed over her cheek. "Too perfect."

A shiver slid over her. "I'm not perfect," Alice said quite clearly as she side-stepped away from Jonathan, making him drop his hand. "And I never claimed to be."

He gave her a brief smile. "So you make mistakes. We all do."

Why was her heart racing so fast? Why was she suddenly nervous to be with him?

He turned away from her and paced toward the window. "Now that the case is over, I guess you won't be seeing Special Agent Zander Todd any longer."

"Actually, I will."

His shoulders stiffened.

It was time to say this. Time to clear the air. "I'm going to keep living."

Jonathan glanced back at her, his brow furrowed. "Of course, you are."

"No, that's not what I—" Alice stopped and pulled in a deep breath. "For the last year, I pulled away from everyone and everything. I retreated to this cabin. I did my freelance work, and I barely had a life. Then Zander came along. He woke me up. He charmed me, and he pissed me off, and he made me see that I can't stay locked away forever. He makes me want more. He makes me want a future, and I'm going to have one."

Now Jonathan turned to fully face her. "With...him?"

Alice nodded. "Yes. Or at least, that's the plan. We're going to try dating." She gave him a weak smile. "Baby steps, you know." Though she felt as if they'd leap-frogged right over the dating deal. Deep inside, Alice knew the truth. She'd fallen hard and fast for her FBI agent. She loved him. A love that scared her because it was already so strong after such a short time. But sometimes, things happened. Things you never planned.

"You're choosing him?"

An odd way to say it, but... "I think we're choosing each other."

Jonathan nodded. "Then I wish you the best, Alice. All I ever wanted was for you to be happy." He came forward and wrapped her in a hug.

Her heart pounded faster. "I-I want you to be happy, too."

He let her go. "I should leave. If the Special Agent is coming back, well, I guess he's going to want to be alone with you."

"It'll be a while before he's here. He has to finish up the paperwork on the case."

Jonathan inclined his head. "I should still go, Alice." He headed for the door. But then he hesitated. Without looking back, he said, "If you're not living in the past, then I shouldn't either. I should let it go. I should let Hugh go."

"It's not your fault." She took a step toward him. "Not the fault of your family. Not the fault of anyone. We make our own choices in this world. Hugh made his choice. He killed. He tortured. Because that was what he wanted to do."

"Yes. I guess that was what he wanted. Time for me to accept that. And it's also time for me to let go. Of him...and of you." He glanced over his shoulder. Wistfully, his gaze swept over her. "Good night, Alice."

The door clicked shut behind him a moment later.

Alice stood there, her hands limp at her sides, as she tried to figure out just why her heart was still racing so fast, why her palms were damp with sweat and why...

Why she was scared.

***

"The reporters were like pit bulls." Randall clapped his hand on Zander's shoulder. "But you handled them like a pro. Way to wrap up this mess."

They were still at the sheriff's station. For the moment, the reporters had backed off. *For the moment.* He and Randall should have been tying up the loose ends for the case, but something kept nagging at Zander. His eyes narrowed as he thought about everything that had happened that night. That fucking twisted night. "How did he know?"

Randall frowned. "Who? What are you talking about?"

"Jonathan Collins. He said that…that I'd tricked Alice. That I'd lied to her." His gut seemed to clench. "How the hell did he know that?"

Randall rocked back as his frown deepened. "Alice must have told him. I mean, they're close, right? I saw him do an interview a while back where he talked about how he still looked out for her. That she was family."

"She's not family," Zander retorted, probably too quickly. "And…no, they hadn't talked in months. Alice told me that. When he came here to the station, that was the first time she'd seen him in over two months." *Right around the same damn time that Julianna Stiles was killed.* Zander replayed things in his mind. "I don't think she told him about how we met. I don't think she told him I was undercover."

Randall blinked. "If she didn't tell him, then how did he find out?"

Zander yanked out his phone. He started to call Alice then remembered—shit, her phone had been collected as evidence. But she would be back at their cabin by now. So he quickly dialed the landline for his place. Only he didn't hear a ringing in his ear. He just got a fast, busy signal.

That twist in his gut became one hell of a lot worse. He turned, roaring out into the station, "I need to reach Deputy Greg Ross right the hell now! Get him on the radio, get me his cell number—*get him!*"

CHAPTER THIRTEEN

Alice hurried into the kitchen and reached for the phone on the counter. It was a landline. Sometimes, cell service was so bad in the mountains that you *had* to use a landline if you wanted to reach anyone. Zander seemed to have better cell service at his place than she did at hers, but since the deputies and agents had confiscated her phone...

Alice reached for the old landline. She picked up the receiver and started to call the station so that she could speak with Zander but—

There was no dial tone. Frowning, she inspected the phone and its cord. The phone was plugged in, it should have been working. Only it wasn't.

Okay, that was weird. Alice hurried back to the front of the cabin. She opened the door. "Deputy Ross!"

The porch was empty.

She crept forward, and the wood groaned beneath her feet. "Deputy Ross?" Alice called again. "I was hoping to use your phone or radio. I need to speak with Zander for a moment." Because all of her instincts were screaming at her. Something was *wrong*. When Jonathan had told her she was "perfect" — her body had instantly tensed. Maybe she was being crazy or hyper paranoid, but so what? She wanted to talk with Zander, wanted to tell him about the suspicion that had slipped into her head.

But she didn't see the deputy.

And she *did* still see Jonathan's car. Only there was no sign of Jonathan near the vehicle.

Oh, shit.

Alice turned and rushed back into the cabin. She locked the front door as fast as she could. Surely, she was wrong. She had to be wrong. Those thoughts rolled through her head again and again even as she rushed into the kitchen and yanked open the drawer near the sink. The drawer that contained utensils. Forks, spoons…knives.

She had to be wrong. Jonathan wasn't a threat to her. His brother had been the killer. Right? *Right?*

Her hand closed around the handle of a knife.

"Alice."

Her head whipped up.

Jonathan stood on the other side of the counter. *Jonathan.*

He smiled at her. "I have a secret for you."

She slid the knife out of the drawer. Kept it at her side.

"My brother loved you. He loved you more than he's ever loved anything in this world. The day he died in that car accident, Hugh was racing to get to the chapel. He was rushing to get there to you because he wanted to tell you something very important."

"Jonathan, how did you get inside?" Because she'd locked the front door when she'd raced back into the cabin.

"I came in the back door. After I knocked out the deputy, I just slipped around and picked the lock. I expected a special agent to have a more secure home." He shrugged. "But I guess this isn't his real home, is it? Just a temporary place. Like you were a temporary case to him."

After I knocked out the deputy. Her knees wanted to buckle, but she stiffened her legs, and she shoved down her fear.

"My brother was coming to tell you something very important," Jonathan continued, as if he just hadn't confessed to assaulting a deputy. "Do you want to know what he was going to say?"

"Y-yes…"

"Hugh was going to tell you…" He put his hands on the counter, and she saw the knife that *he* gripped. "He was going to tell you that he'd just found out I was a killer. That I was cutting up pretty women who looked just...like...you."

***

"What in the fuck is happening, Z?" Randall demanded as Zander's fingers tightened around the steering wheel. They were in an SUV and hauling ass for the cabin. "So the deputy didn't pick up his phone, and his radio was on the fritz, it—"

"Jonathan Collins shouldn't have known that I tricked Alice."

"Uh, okay, but we have the killer. She's on a slab in the morgue, she's—"

"Tiffany wasn't working alone. Shit! The pieces were right in front of me. I didn't see them. Jonathan was there when we talked about getting Alice to wear a wire. He heard our whole fucking plan. That's how Tiffany knew to tell Alice to ditch the wire. Jonathan gave instructions to his partner. He told her what to do, what to say. He told her everything."

Zander took the curve way too fast and the SUV swerved.

"Shit! Slow the hell down!" Randall grabbed the dash board. "Okay, so...what, Jonathan is as crazy as his fool brother? They were working together before Hugh wrapped his car around an electric pole?"

"Maybe." Or…another suspicion, one that had him scared as hell. "Or maybe we had the wrong brother all along. Maybe Hugh Collins wasn't the Secret Admirer."

"A damn body was in his vehicle! He *was* the killer!"

Another curve waited up ahead. Zander was too far from the cabin. Too far. "Just keep trying to get that deputy. And if you reach him — I want Deputy Ross in the cabin with Alice. I want him so close he can touch her, you got me?"

***

Alice felt the skin of her cheeks ice. "You…killed them?"

"Every single one. And it's because of you."

Nausea rose, threatening to choke her.

"I remember the first day Hugh told me about you. I could tell by the way his eyes lit up that you were going to be different. Not like the others at all. You *meant* something to him. And sure enough, days later, he started talking about wanting to marry you. Said you were *perfect*." Jonathan leaned over the counter. "I knew people weren't perfect. My father taught me that. No matter what I did, I could never please him. I was *never* perfect."

She backed away from the counter, keeping her knife tucked behind her jeans. If she could get to the back door, she could run out.

"Then I met you. Saw you and Hugh together." Jonathan's lips twisted in disgust. "I was so fucking mad. You were taking my brother away from me. You were ruining *everything*."

Oh, God. "And you started killing." Those women, over and over—"You started killing me."

"That's how it began, yes. Those women wanted the world to believe they were perfect. But I watched and saw their flaws. And when I saw, they died." He rolled back his shoulders. "I wanted to share their flaws with my brother. I wanted him to realize the truth—so I put the photos in your apartment." He gave a little laugh. "I would sneak into your room all the time, sweet Alice. I wanted to see what Hugh's life was like with you, and I wanted to leave a piece of myself behind."

Because he was fucking crazy.

He inclined his head toward her. "Remember your engagement ring?"

Like she could forget it. "The authorities said it belonged to Mary Ellen Jones."

Mary Ellen had been one of the Secret Admirer's victims.

"It did." He winked at her. "Though I told Hugh it belonged to our great-grandmother.

Damn but I loved seeing that ring on your finger."

She retreated another slow step.

He shoved away from the counter. "But then I started to realize…you actually did seem to love my brother. It was in your eyes. They'd light up, just as his had done. You agreed to marry him. You two started planning your *perfect* life."

She *hated* that word.

"But then, the day of the wedding, Hugh surprised me." His voice roughened. "I mean, he'd practically been living at your apartment, right, so why did he go back to his old place? He shouldn't have gone back. He never should have been there."

She tried to keep her expression blank and not reveal the horror she felt.

Jonathan continued to share his secrets as he said, "Hugh found…evidence, that I'd left behind."

"You were killing in his house?"

Jonathan shrugged. "Of course. I mean, it was empty. Didn't we already fucking establish Hugh spent most of his time with you? So why not use his house? It was a perfect place."

"*Stop* using that word!"

He smiled at her. "I'd stuffed Vicki's body in his SUV. I was planning to ditch her after the wedding, but…well, guess I didn't get around to doing that part, did I? Hugh called me, freaking the hell out. I was at the chapel, with you, like a good brother-in-law to be. I was waiting and he...he was screaming at me. Telling me to get the hell away from you. Telling me he was going to send me to jail. That he'd called the cops, told them to get to his place..." Jonathan's words trailed away. Sadness flickered, then vanished from his face. "My brother didn't realize how guilty he looked. His call to the cops—I'm sure it was frantic. They didn't understand what he was trying to say. Then when he had the accident...and Vicki's body was found..."

Alice slid back one more step. Then another. She was almost at the cabin's rear door.

"My brother died, and I hated that. I *never* wanted Hugh to die." His eyes squeezed shut, only to fly open a moment later. "But the cops stopped looking for the Secret Admirer when he was put into the ground. I was free. So I guess things worked out for me."

Rage and pain burned inside of her.

And Jonathan just smiled. "Then there you were...I have to say, you impressed me. You didn't rush to the reporters. Didn't sell out Hugh. You were true to him, during all those months. Never taking another lover. Proving to me that I had been wrong about you all along. Sweet Alice, you were—"

"I fucked Zander." Her chin notched up. "On the anniversary of Hugh's death, I was in

Zander's bed. I was with him. Because I chose *him* that night."

Jonathan's smile faltered.

"That pissed you off, didn't it? That's why you destroyed my bedroom. That's why you came after me in town—"

"I was protecting you in town. The FBI thought you were guilty. I showed them you weren't. I *helped* you."

The hell he had. "And when you shot the FBI agent—Cara McCoy? Were you *helping* me then?"

But he appeared offended. "I don't kill with guns. Not very personal. I prefer a knife." He glanced down at the weapon he held. "You can feel it when the blade cuts through the skin. Nothing better than that."

Oh, my God.

"I didn't shoot the FBI agent. That was Tiffany. Poor, deluded Tiffany. She wrote to me, did you know that? Sent me long letters telling me how misunderstood she realized my brother had been. Telling me that she was the woman he'd searched to find. That *she* would be perfect...She kept whining about how she wished she'd met the Secret Admirer before his tragic death." He gave a sad shake of his head. "Some people are just sick, you know?"

Yes, she absolutely *knew*.

"So I talked to Tiffany." He shrugged. "Even fucked her a few times. I told her my secrets, and she loved me. She would do anything I wanted. You know, when we fucked, she'd beg me to put the knife at her throat."

She didn't want to hear about them fucking. She wanted away from him. Could she make it out of the door? She was so close...

"Tiffany was an incredible shot, wasn't she? Got to give her credit for that. Tiffany's dad was a cop, the guy taught her how to shoot before she could even tie her shoes. She was lethal. And crazy as hell. That's probably why she killed her dad when she turned sweet sixteen. But hey, I killed my old man, too. Did it when I was just ten years old. Shoved the bastard down the stairs, and no one ever knew."

She tried to keep her breathing steady. Another step back—

"Alice..." He shook his head. "That door is locked. You're not getting away from me. I've waited a long time to have you."

"To kill me."

He gave another shrug. "I was going to love you. But...like you said, you chose the special agent." His eyes glittered at her. "You made the *wrong* choice."

Her hold on the hidden knife tightened. "I don't think I did."

He lunged toward her, slashing out with his knife, but she ducked, and then she surged up with her blade. She didn't slice. She *shoved* that blade into his side as hard as she could. Jonathan grunted and stared at her with wide eyes in a tense moment that seemed to last forever.

"Alice…" He stumbled back.

She whirled for the back door. Her fingers were shaking as she flipped up the lock, then wrenched open the door. Alice rushed onto the steps that would lead to freedom. She was —

He tackled her. He hit her hard, and they fell onto the ground with so much force that the air was driven from her lungs. She couldn't even scream as he twisted her around, rolling her over and shoving a knife to her throat.

"You don't…" His breath heaved out. "Get to run."

The knife cut into her skin, and Alice finally got the breath to scream. She screamed as loud as she could.

The knife cut her harder. "No one can hear you. The deputy is out cold…or, hell, he could be dead. I didn't check. Your FBI agent…" He grunted. "You told me he's in the town for a while. Just you and me. You and —"

Her hand slid down to his side. He'd yanked out the knife she'd put in him, but she could feel the wetness of his blood beneath her touch, so Alice knew she'd located the wound. Alice jabbed her fingers into the wound as hard as she could.

He bellowed, his grip on her easing as he cried out in pain, and the knife at her throat lifted for one frantic moment. She twisted and lunged away from him, rising to her feet and staggering away.

"You *bitch!*"

She ran around the side of the cabin. And as she did, Alice heard the growl of an engine approaching. A car—someone coming to help! She just had to get to the front of the cabin. Had to get the attention of whoever was arriving. "Help me!" Alice yelled. So close. She was almost there! A few more feet and she'd be in front of the cabin. "Help—"

Jonathan's arms wrapped around her as he yanked her back against his body. She twisted, but he just turned and slammed her head into the side of the cabin, momentarily stunning her.

Then she felt the knife press to her throat once more. "You won't call out again. Not a single fucking sound, or I will slit you open from ear to ear."

Brakes squealed, and car doors slammed. The vehicle was in front of the cabin. She was hidden on the left side.

"Not a sound," Jonathan whispered. "Or you die."

"*Alice!*" The cry of her name filled the night. Furious and desperate. Zander's voice.

"Just check the cabin!" Another male shouted at him. *Randall.* "She's probably inside, safe and sound, and you're being a total nutjob."

"Where's the fucking deputy then?" Zander's steps rushed onto the wooden porch. "And did you *see* the other car out front?" She heard the jingle of keys and then—

"When they go inside," Jonathan's breath blew over her ear as he murmured to her, his words barely distinguishable, *"we'll get in my car. We'll get the hell out of here."*

No, no, they wouldn't. If she got in that car, she was dead. Alice knew it. Hell, he might even just kill her as soon as Zander and Randall entered the cabin. Then Zander would have to find her body later.

It wasn't going to happen. She wasn't getting into Jonathan's car. And she wasn't going to be helpless. Zander was close. She just had to get Jonathan's hand off her mouth. If she called out, Zander would help her.

Alice jabbed her elbow back at Jonathan's ribs as hard as she could.

He gave a grunt, but Jonathan didn't let her go.

She shoved down on his foot, grinding with her heel.

Still won't free me.

The knife was cutting into her throat.

"Enough," Jonathan rasped, "stop it, you—"

Her right hand flew up. She didn't try to grab his whole hand — the hand that pressed over her mouth. Instead, she just went for his pinky finger. Exactly like she'd been taught in her self-defense classes. Did he know that she'd taken them? After everything that had gone down, hell, *yes,* she'd taken them. So she went for his pinky because it was the most fragile part of his hand. She grabbed it and wrenched back, snapping those delicate bones.

He yelled.

So did she. Actually, Alice screamed. She screamed as loud as she could even though the knife was still at her throat. "*Zander! Don't go in the cabin! I'm here, I'm —* "

"Dead!" Jonathan snarled. The knife's blade bit into the flesh under her left ear. He was going to slice her, from ear to ear, just as he'd warned.

But a bright light hit them.

"*Get the fuck away from her!*" Zander's roar. And she could just see him past the light. It was a flashlight that he held, one that was positioned above his gun.

"You're going to watch her die!" Jonathan shouted at Zander. "See her bleed out and you won't be able to do a damn thing to stop her death!"

"Really?" Zander's voice had gone flat and cold. "That's what you think? You're *dead* wrong.

Alice isn't dying because I'm about to shoot *you* right between the eyes."

"Bullshit! You won't take the shot!" Jonathan denied. His spittle flew against Alice's cheek. "You won't risk shooting her!"

"I'm a fucking fine shot," Zander threw out in his lethal voice. "And the only one dying tonight is you. I will have that bullet between your eyes long before your knife can sink into her skin. I'll fire, and I'll be the last damn thing you see before you open your eyes to hell. Do you understand me?"

"If you could take the shot, you would have done it!" Rage shook Jonathan's voice and body. "You're bluffing! Drop your weapon! Drop it, *now!*"

"Don't...Zander, don't," Alice pleaded.

The flashlight didn't waver, but...Zander dropped the gun.

"Good." Satisfaction purred from Jonathan. "Now you can watch as—"

"I wasn't bluffing," Zander cut in, his words a fierce growl. "I was stalling. There's a difference, you see. I was stalling so that my partner could sneak up behind your dumb ass. And guess what? *He's there.*"

She felt the shock roll through Jonathan. He jerked and then he spun around, yanking her with him, but Alice stumbled, deliberately, and as her body slumped to the side, the knife's blade wasn't pressed to her skin any longer. She was clear for a few precious moments —

"Drop the fucking knife!" Randall thundered. Then...

Boom. Boom.

The explosion rang in her ears right before Alice's body was suddenly free. She tumbled onto the ground, then immediately scrambled up, running for safety, running for Zander.

He caught her, yanking her into his arms and holding her tight. "God, baby...*God.*" His hold was so fierce and hard that she could barely breathe.

Then Zander was pushing her behind him. He grabbed his gun and advanced on the fallen man. Randall still had his weapon and flashlight aimed at Jonathan's body.

"Stay down," Randall ordered Jonathan.

He's still alive. Jonathan's body was shaking. The knife was a few inches from his hand.

And she realized he wasn't going to stay down. She had that realization right before Jonathan grabbed for the knife and lunged —

Randall and Zander both fired. This time, when Jonathan fell back, his body wasn't shaking. He wasn't moving at all.

"Told you," Zander said quietly. "The only one dying tonight...it's you."

***

A swirl of blue and red lights illuminated the cabin. Zander marched past the FBI agents and the deputies and headed straight for the ambulance. One ambulance had already left, taking Deputy Greg Ross to the hospital. The guy was going to be all right, once he got over the concussion he'd received.

The second ambulance's back doors were open, and Zander overheard the EMT say, "Are you sure you don't want to go to the hospital, ma'am? You could use a few stitches—"

"I'm not leaving Zander." Alice jumped from the ambulance. He could see the bandages that had been placed on her neck. *To cover the wounds from that bastard's knife.*

Alice turned her head, and her gaze locked on Zander. A smile curved her beautiful lips as she hurtled toward him. He caught her, locking her tightly against him, and then he kissed her, not giving one flying fuck about who might notice them. Reporters were already on scene. The *real* Secret Admirer had been unmasked — and killed. No way would this story not make every news show in the United States.

"I was so damn scared," he whispered those words. Words that were only for her. "I kept thinking that I wouldn't get to you in time. If he'd killed you…" Zander couldn't finish that sentence. If Alice had died, Zander feared he might have gone crazy. Fucking insane.

She stared up at him. "It's over. Really over now."

"The case is over. We're not."

She smiled at him. "No, we're not. You owe me a whole lot of dates."

"A lifetime of them." If that was what she wanted. He'd give her *anything* she wanted. "Alice May, God, I love you." He stared at her, so grateful she was alive and safe in his arms. "And maybe one day, you'll love me, too."

She kissed him, then pulled back as she said, "I already do."

He was sure he'd misheard her. No way, no way would Alice—

"I love you, Zander Todd. And I'm ready for dates. I'm ready for anything but death. I want to see what happens with us. Every wild thing that can come our way. I want to be happy, and I want to be with you."

Yes, oh, hell, *yes.* He pulled her tightly against him. Took her mouth. Then he rasped against her lips, "You're the only thing I want."

Now and forever, it would always be Alice for him.

His Alice. Brave. Strong. Smart. Sexy.

The woman who'd taught an FBI agent that there was more to life than just cases. So much more.

He looked at Alice, and knew...she was his everything.

Now and forever.

EPILOGUE

"Are you sure this is what you want?"
Zander's handsome face showed his worry.

But Alice just smiled at him. "Absolutely."
She smoothed her hand over her soft cream dress.
There was no bouquet this time. No chapel full of
people waiting.

No fear.

"I love you," he said. And she knew he did.
She could see the love when he looked at her. His
face would soften, his lips would curl.

And she loved him. She loved him more than
she would have ever thought possible. They'd
been together six months. Six wonderful months
and now...

The music began to play.

"I thought we were just coming to Vegas for
a vacation," Zander murmured.

Yes, Alice knew Zander had thought
that...until she'd asked *him* to marry her. He'd
agreed instantly, with a "Hell, yes!"

The chapel doors opened. The place had an
Elvis theme, and she thought it was perfect. They

walked down the aisle together, because that was how their life worked. *Together.*

Alice's gaze slid to Zander. She found him already watching her. His expression had softened, and the love—it was so easy to see.

"Forever, Alice," he told her.

And she knew that's exactly what she was going to get—forever, with the man who loved her. Turned out, Alice had been very, very lucky in her life. Hugh Collins hadn't been a killer. He'd been a man who loved her, who wanted to protect her. Finally knowing the truth had changed Alice's life. She'd grieved for Hugh, for the good man that he'd been. For the life they could've had. And Zander had been with her. Supporting her. Loving her. Every moment.

She'd lost Hugh, but she'd gotten a second chance. Second chances didn't happen often, and Alice knew how incredibly fortunate she was. Alice was so glad that she'd opened her heart to Zander.

She was happy again. She could love again. She could live again.

And that was exactly what she planned to do…with her special agent.

With her husband.

"Forever, Zander," she murmured back to him.

Zander's hand took hers, and their new life began.

The End

A NOTE FROM THE AUTHOR

Thank you so much for reading SECRET ADMIRER! When this story slipped into my mind, I couldn't wait to share Alice's life with you. I love the idea of second chances, and I felt like Alice deserved one. Sometimes, things aren't what they appear, and I'm always interested in looking past the surface to see what secrets are waiting to be discovered.

If you'd like to stay updated on my releases and sales, please join my newsletter list.

http://www.cynthiaeden.com/newsletter/

Again, thank you for reading SECRET ADMIRER.

Best,
Cynthia Eden
www.cynthiaeden.com

ABOUT THE AUTHOR

Award-winning author Cynthia Eden writes dark tales of paranormal romance and romantic suspense. She is a New York Times, USA Today, Digital Book World, and IndieReader best-seller. Cynthia is also a three-time finalist for the RITA® award. Since she began writing full-time in 2005, Cynthia has written over eighty novels and novellas.

For More Information

- *www.cynthiaeden.com*
- *http://www.facebook.com/cynthiaedenfanpage*
- *http://www.twitter.com/cynthiaeden*

HER OTHER WORKS

Romantic Suspense
Lazarus Rising

- Never Let Go (Book One, Lazarus Rising)
- Keep Me Close (Book Two, Lazarus Rising)
- Stay With Me (Book Three, Lazarus Rising)
- Run To Me (Book Four, Lazarus Rising)
- Lie Close To Me (Book Five, Lazarus Rising)
-

Dark Obsession Series

- Watch Me (Dark Obsession, Book 1)
- Want Me (Dark Obsession, Book 2)
- Need Me (Dark Obsession, Book 3)
- Beware Of Me (Dark Obsession, Book 4)
- Only For Me (Dark Obsession, Books 1 to 4)

Mine Series

- Mine To Take (Mine, Book 1)
- Mine To Keep (Mine, Book 2)
- Mine To Hold (Mine, Book 3)
- Mine To Crave (Mine, Book 4)
- Mine To Have (Mine, Book 5)
- Mine To Protect (Mine, Book 6)
- Mine Series Box Set Volume 1 (Mine, Books 1-3)
- Mine Series Box Set Volume 2 (Mine, Books 4-6)

Other Romantic Suspense

- First Taste of Darkness
- Sinful Secrets
- Until Death
- Christmas With A Spy

Paranormal Romance
Bad Things

- The Devil In Disguise (Bad Things, Book 1)
- On The Prowl (Bad Things, Book 2)
- Undead Or Alive (Bad Things, Book 3)
- Broken Angel (Bad Things, Book 4)
- Heart Of Stone (Bad Things, Book 5)
- Tempted By Fate (Bad Things, Book 6)
- Bad Things Volume One (Books 1 to 3)
- Bad Things Volume Two (Books 4 to 6)

- Bad Things Deluxe Box Set (Books 1 to 6)
- Wicked And Wild (Bad Things, Book 7)

Bite Series

- Forbidden Bite (Bite Book 1)
- Mating Bite (Bite Book 2)

Blood and Moonlight Series

- Bite The Dust (Blood and Moonlight, Book 1)
- Better Off Undead (Blood and Moonlight, Book 2)
- Bitter Blood (Blood and Moonlight, Book 3)
- Blood and Moonlight (The Complete Series)

Purgatory Series

- The Wolf Within (Purgatory, Book 1)
- Marked By The Vampire (Purgatory, Book 2)
- Charming The Beast (Purgatory, Book 3)
- Deal with the Devil (Purgatory, Book 4)
- The Beasts Inside (Purgatory, Books 1 to 4)

Bound Series

- Bound By Blood (Bound Book 1)
- Bound In Darkness (Bound Book 2)
- Bound In Sin (Bound Book 3)
- Bound By The Night (Bound Book 4)
- Forever Bound (Bound, Books 1 to 4)
- Bound in Death (Bound Book 5)

11707053R00125

Made in the USA
Lexington, KY
14 October 2018